中文裡有句話說「好事成雙」。我的系列書現在也進行到第十七和第十八本，也是兩本一套。這兩本彼此相呼應，一本講的是自然，另一本講文化，有時候這兩件事的界線有點模糊，沒法清楚的界定。

很幸運地，我對中文跟英文有足夠的理解，雖然程度可能不是很深，但總是用中英文雙語呈現。有些時候翻譯沒有辦法做到完全貼切，畢竟每一種語言都有它獨特的微妙跟幽默。但是我盡力讓它們的意思貼切。

我可以空下來專心寫作的時間其實很有限。也因為我給寫作這樣少的時間，所以我從不會把自己看待成一個專業的作家。但是我非常珍惜寫作的時間，它讓我可以去紀錄，回顧，思考，同時也天馬行空，從事實到想像。

對我來說，寫作是心甘情願的事，也是浪漫的時刻。但是出書卻是另一回事，痛苦肯定少不了，或許有點像生小孩。我通常習慣用十個月去醞釀，寫作，然後兩個月生產。

如果書是小孩的話，我現在有兩打左右的孩子，每一個對我來說都是獨一無二的、可愛的，每一個都有自己的個性，每個都很寶貴。有些書即使是多年前出版的，但我希望沒有一本會感覺很老。

希望你會喜歡新的這一對。

There is a Chinese saying; "Good things come in pairs". So maybe it is fitting that my books, now into the 17th and 18th of a series, are again released as a pair. They always complement each other, with one on nature and the other on culture, though at times the line is a bit blurry and not defined in an absolute way.

I am also blessed with a reasonable understanding of both English and Chinese. Thus my books always come with another set of pairing, bilingual in Chinese and English. At times it is not a fully perfect translation, as each language carries its own subtlety and humor. But try I must, to make my writing relevant in its meaning and context.

The time I can spare for writing is quite limited. In no way can I consider myself a professional writer, given the small fraction of time I allot to such vocation. That time, however, is what I find most precious, as it allows my mind to record, reflect, as well as to wander, from the factual to the imaginative.

For me writing is a labor of love, a time of romance. Producing a book however is another kind of labor, not without pain and perhaps a bit like delivering a baby. My usual routine is ten months of gestation in writing, then two months of labor for delivery.

If books are like babies, I now have around two dozen, and each one to me is unique, lovely, with its own character, and precious. And I hope none would feel old, even if I have created them many years ago.

Please enjoy this new pair of twins.

Authored and Photographed by Wong How Man

NATURE MY FATE

自然
緣份

黃效文—

著

序

摯友黃效文兄出版自然文化新書二冊，囑咐小弟撰寫序言。小弟久未執筆，不知從何寫起，自己在問，究竟如何初次認識效文？腦波頻動，立時走進時光隧道。

時維一九九九年，正值金秋，邀得黃效文兄替小弟公司拍攝數碼攝錄機電視廣告宣傳片，故事內容簡潔，展示此激情探險家喜愛備帶 Panasonic 數碼攝錄機，周遊歷險，紀錄澎湃江河、崇山峻嶺、壯觀原野等景象。十分肯定，從此以後，吾兄一直使用著小弟代理品牌之攝錄機、電飯煲、手提電話、冷氣機、雪櫃等等，不一而足。如今吾兄府上，眾多工作據點，誠像小弟代理品牌之產品陳列室也。

效文兄乃吾一生之中遇見以探險事業為生第一人，絕非兒時所閱歷險故事所述泛泛之輩。探索奇峰異洞、涉獵名山大川、駕馭越野戰車、馳騁於密林沙漠之間之一般探險家歷練，吾兄定必經歷無數。

當吾隨效文兄造訪其重建之修道院，方知吾兄一以探險，

FOREWORD

When How Man asked me to write a foreword for his two new books, I asked myself, "When did I first meet How Man? How did I get to know him?" My memory immediately went through the time tunnel; it was sometime in the fall of 1999. My company wanted to ask him to help promote on TV a product that he has been using in rather extreme conditions in the field . The storyline was very simple. It was about this very passionate explorer, Wong How Man, who loved to use a Panasonic Movie Camera.

I am pretty sure that it was from that moment onward that How Man started to use my movie cameras, my rice cookers, my mobile phones, my air conditioners, my refrigerators, etc., etc., And now, his homes and all his sites look just like my showrooms.

For me, it was my first time to encounter a person who made his career in exploration. How Man is not the usual explorer that I read about in story books when I was a kid. Of course, I am sure that he has crawled inside many caves, climbed many mountains and sped his Land Rover through many jungles and deserts. When he took me to the nunnery that he restored, however, I was

一以復修；當吾手抱效文兄試從英國帶回緬甸之緬甸貓，方才得知吾兄尚且保育稀有品種動物；當吾見證效文兄引薦二位來自古巴老婦，詠唱粵曲於香港石澳文物古屋之中，吾對效文兄工作所觸及領域之廣闊，甚感嘆為觀止。效文兄尋幽訪勝，時有驚人發現，每每給人帶來意外驚喜。

效文吾兄，擇善固執，探險精神，堅持不渝！小弟樂於偶爾奉陪，攜手踏上征途。

蒙德揚

中國探險學會 董事會成員
二零一六年十月

Mr. David Mong with Burmese kittens / 蒙德揚先生與緬甸幼貓

amazed that he not only explored, he also restored. When I held those Burmese Cats that he purchased from the United Kingdom, I then learned that he was preserving this endangered breed and was bringing them back home to Burma. When I saw the Chinese Opera performance by the two old Cuban ladies in Shek O, I was stunned once again by the scope of work of How Man.

Wong How Man always surprises me with his new "findings". Keep up with the good work pal. I promise that I will join you on expedition again soon.

David Mong

Member of the Board
China Exploration and Research Society
October 2016

欽敦貓 CHINDWIN FELINE

Masein, Sagaing State, Myanmar - December 3, 2014

欽敦貓

我受夠了！我要找隻貓！老鼠啃我的船，真的在吃我的船！我的充氣橡皮艇。

坐了九小時的吉普車，從 *Monywa* 到 *Kalewa*，再到欽敦江上游，欽敦江是伊洛瓦底江的主要支流，而我在昨天傍晚才終於登上 *HM Explorer*。今天早上我發現我們的一艘充氣橡皮艇變成了一堆橡膠布那樣的攤開在甲板上，而工作人員正在修補被咬破的地方。

老鼠吃掉了船身中間的管，也就是船的脊骨，這些破洞很大，不是我們用強力膠就可以補救的。我不知道 *PVC* 吃起來味道怎樣，但是這些老鼠肯定是餓慌了，連這麼硬的橡膠也吃。每個破洞大約有二到四吋長，大概兩吋寬。

貓，我可不能隨便找。畢竟 *CERS* 可是被認為是緬甸貓的爺爺。在國際上，大家都知道是我們把緬甸貓帶回緬甸的。但是，這種尊貴的貓咪可是不會去追可惡的老鼠，這

CHINDWIN FELINE

I've had IT! I'm going to get a cat. The mice have been chewing up my boat! Literally eating my boat! My Zodiac inflatable boat, that is.

I boarded the HM Explorer yesterday evening after a long nine-hour ride on a jeep, bouncing from Monywa to Kalewa, toward the upper reaches of the Chindwin River, a major tributary of the Irrawaddy. This morning, I found one of our two Zodiac boats was laid on the upper deck, stretched out as a pile of rubber, as the crew was trying to repair the leak.

A major leak it was, not something we could just put a patch to and fix with superglue. The mice had eaten up two sections of the center tube which acted as the keel to the boat. I have no idea what PVC tasted like, but the mice must be have been starving to devour such hard plastic. Each hole was between two to four inches long and maybe two inches wide.

But I could not just get any cat. After all, CERS is considered grandfather of the Burmese Cat. We are known internationally to have reintroduced this important breed back to Myanmar. But then, royal cats don't go after

些貓咪都是等著被人餵食的。所以我們只能找欽敦貓，有貓界的「駄馬」之稱，真的會抓老鼠來吃。

我計畫要去一個叫 Masein 的小鎮已經好一段時間，那是一個很漂亮又乾淨的小鎮，在欽敦旁，離上游約四小時。我猜想，Masein 的貓應該也是一樣美麗又乾淨。我們在中午前抵達了那裏。我們最新一期季刊的封面就是 Masein，一隻狗帶領著一群人進城。他們的貓咪應該也不差，我猜一定很特別。

我走進一間由年輕女士打理的理髮店，準備剪頭髮跟刮鬍子。也趁這機會讓我靜靜的思考一下關於貓的事。如果船上的老鼠都被消滅光了，只有一隻貓在船上可能會感覺孤寂。所以我們一定要有兩隻貓，兩隻同一胎的小貓，從小就玩在一起，他們互相作伴。

理髮店旁邊是金匠舖子。村長 Win Shwe 剛好在店裡，我跟他聊了起來。他馬上說可以幫我們找到兩隻小貓，一公一母。在等待村長把貓咪帶來的時間，我們在小鎮上散步，街道很乾淨，也逛了市場，一樣很乾淨，但是空蕩蕩的。早市在熱帶地區好像只有一個鐘頭的營業時間。很快村長回來了，拎著一只裝著兩隻小貓的塑膠籃子。

我往籃子裡探，看見兩隻小貓，一隻毛色比另外一隻金

Win Shwe delivering cats / Win Shwen（藍衣男）把貓咪送來

the lowly mice. They are simply fed. So a Chindwin cat we must resort to, something that is a workhorse of a cat, hungry enough to hunt and fetch its own food.

I had been planning to stop by a small, beautiful and clean town called Masein by the Chindwin, and it was only four hours away upriver. Masein cats might just be as clean and beautiful. By noon, we landed in Masein. Our latest newsletter has Masein on its cover, with a picture of a dog leading a parade through town. Their cats must not be far behind, something special I assume.

I had my haircut and a clean shave at a small barber shop run by a young

黃。"哈囉！ *Hello Kitties*" 我對牠們喵。啊哈！我馬上幫牠們取好名字。哈囉的緬甸話，我唯一會講的一句 *"Min-galaba"*。所以男生叫 *Minga*，女生叫 *Laba*。用緬甸話的哈囉來命名我們的 *Hello Kitties*，配的多巧妙！

我們問村長要付他多少錢，「免費！」他回答。「但是我想要你們的季刊」，村長接著說。他很驚訝我們學會季刊封面上的照片有著他熟悉的面孔，而且就來自他的鎮，內頁還有許多這個鎮的照片。成交！但是我們還是給了村長一筆豐厚的小費感謝他的協助。

乘船旅行讓我有機會可以好好的閱讀之前沒有時間看的書。我帶了幾本雜誌、期刊和書上船，像是 *FP*〈*Foreign Policy*〉，*East*，義大利的地理政治刊物，經濟學人，彭

lady. It provided idle time to contemplate about the cat. One would be too lonely on the boat, once the mice had been eradicated. So we must have two cats, two kittens from the same litter that are used to playing with each other and keeping good company.

Next to the barber shop was a goldsmith's shop. The village chief Win Shwe happened to be there and we started a conversation. In no time he hurried off to locate two kittens for us. I wanted one male and one female. In the mean time we strolled down the very tidy streets and visited the now empty, yet clean, market place. Morning markets only lasted an hour or so in such tropical area. Soon the Chief arrived with a plastic basket holding two kittens.

I took a peek inside and saw two kitties, one slightly lighter golden than the other. "Hello, hello kitties," so I meowed out. Aha, momentarily I got the names for our kitties. Hello in Burmese, and the only Burmese that I can speak, is Mingalaba. So the boy would be Minga, and the girl Laba. Burmese greeting names for our Hello Kitties, how appropriate and matching!

We asked Win Shwe how much to pay for the cats. "Free," he answered. "I would like the newsletter in return," said Win Shwe. He was impressed with the cover with familiar faces from his town, and an inside story having more pictures from around town. We struck a deal, but added a generous tip for

Chicken vender heading for market / 前往市場的雞販

his effort.

The boat trip is always an excellent opportunity for me to catch up on all the readings I have been longing for during the previous months. So getting on board with me were several magazines, journals and books. FP (Foreign Policy), East, a geopolitical journal published in Italy, and the Economist and Bloomberg are standard issues. Not least the high drama and gossip of Vanity Fair, though there are always some well-researched articles thrown in.

The current Vanity Fair, being a thick December shoppers' issue, was too weighty to lug around while transiting airports to Myanmar. Thus came off, by tearing, 78 pages of double-page advertisements. That effectively took the magazine to half its thickness and weight, without diluting the main articles and their juicy spices.

It was not too comforting that one of the main stories in the December issue of Vanity Fair is about boat salvaging in the open sea. The author noted that of approximately 100,000 ships plying the ocean globally today, a quarter would be lost within the next decade. Though he was writing about

博這類的雜誌。還有誇張八卦的＜浮華世界＞，其實裡面有幾篇文章的研究做的蠻好的。

最新一期的＜浮華世界＞裡夾有一本購物指南，很厚，拎著它去緬甸，又要轉機，實在是太重了，所以有七十八頁的跨頁廣告都被我撕掉了。這個方法很有效的把雜誌的厚度跟重量減半，又不用犧牲主要的內容跟它們好看的地方。

＜浮華世界＞十二月份的這期裡面有一篇文章讓我看了不是很舒服，它說的是在外海打撈沈船。作者提到現今大約有 *100,000* 艘船在全球行駛，四分之一的船在未來的十年會消失掉。雖然他說的是海運，儘管如此，我還是有點焦慮，因為未來的三周我將會住在船上。

在由曼谷飛往緬甸的飛機上，*Bill* 轉過來問我，入境表上的住宿地點要寫哪裡。要跟海關解釋清楚 *HM Explorer*（我們探險船的名字）是什麼，是件複雜的事。「照舊，我一向都是填最昂貴的飯店，確定他們一定會尊敬禮遇你。」我這樣告訴*Bill*。「就寫 *The Strand* 或是 *Inle Princess*」我說。

關於職業，我會視情況而改變我的答案。*Daniel Ng*，已經過世的 *CERS* 主席，他最有名的是在職業欄填「坦克指揮官」，而不是麥當勞董事長。最近進入緬甸我可以在職業欄填「專門搞定事的人」或是「幫成龍勘景的人」，

maritime shipping, I am nonetheless somewhat apprehensive, having to live on a boat for the next three weeks.

While in flight from Bangkok to Mandalay, Bill turned around to me seated behind him and asked what to put in the immigration form column that asked where we would be staying. Certainly we couldn't explain all the complexity by filling in "HM Explorer", the name of our boat. "As a rule, I always put the most expensive hotel. That way, you are sure to command some respect," I told Bill as a matter of fact. "Just write down The Strand, or the Inle Princess," I added.

Laba found her nest / Laba 找到牠的窩

畢竟他在緬甸比我們香港特首還有名，也勝過中國的習主席。

如果海關對我填寫的有任何質疑，我的 *iPad* 裡面有一套三十秒的影片，成龍剛拍給 *CERS* 的公益宣傳片。宣傳影片的內容是請求緬甸人不要在依洛瓦底江裡電魚，依洛瓦底江裡的海豚快要絕種了，牠們需要被保護。成龍在片中還說了幾句緬甸話來吸引觀眾注意。他說的第一個字 *"Mingalaba"*，算是對我們新來的貓 *"Minga"* 跟 *"Laba"* 最貼切的致敬。

Minga and Laba / Minga 和 Laba

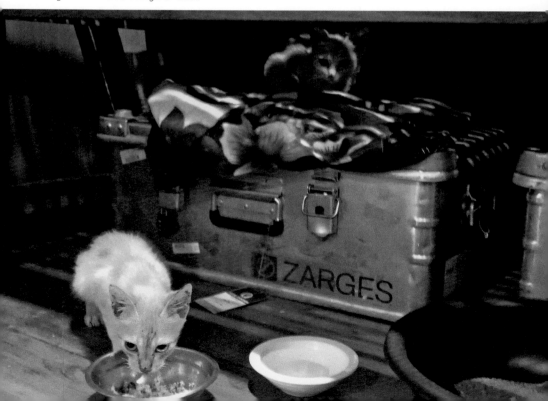

As with profession, I wrote whatever I felt like being each time depending on the different circumstances. Daniel Ng, late CERS Chairman, was known to put his profession as a "tank commander", rather than as Chairman of McDonald's Restaurant. These days, entering Myanmar I can list myself as a fixer or someone scouting for location for Jackie Chan's next film. After all, he is far more famous here in Myanmar than our Chief Executive in Hong Kong, and as a matter of fact, more so than President Xi of China.

And if the immigration officer should doubt my claim, my iPad has a newly finished 30-second video that Jackie Chan has just recorded for CERS, to be used as a social media message. It is a message calling on the Burmese to stop electro-fishing on the Irrawaddy in order to save the endangered Irrawaddy Dolphin. He even spoke a couple of sentences in Burmese language to impress his viewers. And Jackie's first remark was, "Mingalaba", a most appropriate tribute to our two new cats, Minga and Laba.

伊洛瓦底江的一場高潮

HIGH DRAMA ON THE IRRAWADDY

Mandalay, Myanmar – April 5, 2015

伊洛瓦底江的一場高潮

CERS 打擊流氓組織

這男人輕輕的把門打開，踮著腳尖走在 *HM Explorer* 的下甲板，*106* 呎河船，CERS 用來當作我們在緬甸兩條最大的淡水河上做研究的船。他查覺到所有的船艙門都關著，所以他輕輕的走了幾步進到船上的用餐區。燈光微弱，但是他帶著手電筒，用很快的速度掃射桌面。

收穫挺不賴的一晚，好幾支手機，還有幾個看起來夠科技的東西應該值些錢。他可能並不知道那是電腦的硬碟，把它們通通塞進包包裡。*iPad* 在桌上，他也不知道那是什麼東西，管他的，先塞進去再說。接下來他抓到一個放在桌下的背包，此刻他聽到聲音從船艙裡傳來，於是趕緊奪門而出，消失在黑夜裡，在依洛瓦底江中段的一個堤壩上岸。

就在他要離開船的時候，看見了幾個大包包在船首，他的搭檔在外面等著，他們把其中一個包包拉上岸。剖開包包，往裡面瞧，只看到一堆一模一樣的 *T-shirt*，上面印著像魚的圖案，他很快的把它們丟在一旁，繼續往裡面挖

HIGH DRAMA ON THE IRRAWADDY

CERS as gang buster

The man opened the door softly and tiptoed onto the lower deck of HM Explorer, the 106-foot riverboat CERS uses as our research vessel on the two largest freshwater rivers of Myanmar. He noticed all the cabin doors were closed, so he gingerly took a few more steps and entered the main dining area of the boat. The lights were dim, but he had a flash light with him, which he shined quickly on the tables.

Not a bad night; there were several mobile phones sitting around and a few more devices that looked technical enough to be worth something. While he didn't know those were hard drives for computers, he stuffed them into his sack nonetheless. There was an iPad on the table. He didn't quite understand what that was either, but what the hell, stuff it in first. Next he grabbed a backpack from under the table. Momentarily he heard some sound coming from one of the cabins. Quickly he rushed out the door and disappeared into the dark night onto a sandbar in the middle of the Irrawaddy River.

But just as he was leaving the boat, he saw huge bags lying on the bow. With

寶。他從船上帶走的那個包包裡面還有很多好東西，一支電話，一個硬碟，一個 Kindle。他從沒見過像 iPad 跟 Kindle 這樣的東西，但是它們看起來夠搶眼，也許他覺得那可能是某種手提電視吧。

沒人知道我們被偷了，直到 Berry 四點半起床開始她的一天。這是她的習慣，即使在香港，緬甸的時間比香港晚一個半鐘頭。她找不到她的電話，硬碟，但是想想她可能把它們忘在船上的哪個地方。接近六點的時候，我們的大副比手畫腳的跟我們示意，他在沙灘上找到 Camilla 的背包，還有我們放 T-shirt 的大包包。

此刻，我們才知道我們被小偷光顧了。Camilla 最慘，她聖誕節在英國媽媽送她的 Kindle 被偷了，還有一台存放她所有舊照片的硬碟也不見了。Camilla 是我們的大象專家，硬碟上還有很多資料。Berry 也好不到哪裡去，掉了三支手機，還有一個 iPad 已經夠糟了，最後發現連兩個硬碟也被偷了。

我們馬上派上一艘充氣橡皮艇去鄰近的明宮（Mingun）報警，那裏距離曼德勒坐船約四十五分鐘，是個觀光景點。到了八點，四位警察登上我們的船蒐證做口供報告。他們在沙灘上來回走，發現有昨晚留下的新腳印。拍下犯罪現場照片。很明顯的應該有三到四個小偷，搭小船

one partner who was waiting outside, they hauled one of these to the sand. There he slit open the bag. When he looked inside and only found identical T-shirts with something like a fish on it, he quickly threw these aside and continued with his rummaging. The backpack he had taken from the boat, however, yielded yet more goodies; another phone, a hard drive, and a Kindle. He had never seen devices like an iPad and Kindle but they looked interesting enough for the grab. Perhaps they were some kind of portable TV, so he thought.

The theft wasn't noticed until 4:30 am when Berry woke up to begin her day of work. That was her routine even in Hong Kong, though here in Myanmar the time was one and a half hours behind that of Hong Kong. She couldn't find her phones and hard drives but thought perhaps they had been left somewhere else on the boat. Then, before 6am, our First Mate ran in gesturing that he had found Camilla's backpack on the sandy shore, as well as one of our large bags of T-shirts.

By then, we knew we had been patronized by thieves. Camilla was the most miserable, losing her Kindle given to her by her mother over Christmas in the UK, and also all of her old photos on her hard drives. Camilla is our elephant expert and she also had a lot of data on her hard drives. Berry likewise found the loss of her two hard drives even more inconvenient than losing three mobile phones and an iPad.

偷摸上我們的船。

也許沒有面遇小偷們是幸運的，因為他們很可能會帶傢伙。但是我很快的跟大家說緬甸基本上還是安全的，只是我們要小心一點。小偷到處都有，小心謹慎點就是了。睡前把船艙的門都鎖上、重要的東西一定要收好，成為了我們的新規矩。另外，船上的十位工作人員還有員工，也開始輪流帶著手電筒巡邏。我甚至在想是不是要裝可以偵測動作的照明跟攝影機，但是想想還是作罷，我不想把我們的船搞的好像一艘武裝的河船。這樣會變的很不好玩。

Police approaching our boat / 警察的橡皮艇正向我們的船駛來

We immediately sent one of our Zodiacs off to make a police report at nearby Mingun, a tourist site within 45 minutes boat journey from Mandalay. By 8am, four policemen boarded our boat to file the report and take evidence. They paced the sandy shore and noticed fresh footprints left from the night. Pictures were taken of the crime scene. Obviously the thieves, maybe three to four, had come on shore in a small boat and sneaked onto our boat.

Perhaps it was lucky that we did not accost them, as they might have been armed. I soon reminded everyone that, while Myanmar is generally safe, we must be prepared. Petty theft may happen anywhere, and we all need to be more careful in the future. Locking the boat doors at night and putting away our valuables became our policy from then on. As we have up to ten boat crew and staff, they too would maintain more vigilance and make occasional night rounds with flash lights. I even thought of installing motion detector activated lights and cameras, but decided against making our boat like an armed battleship on the river. That would take away a lot of the fun.

After that unfortunate episode, we cruised on and continued on our journey, including flying off to our Inle Lake project site for a quick inspection. We talked to the police, and they thought there was little chance of cracking the case and finding the lost items. However, things developed unexpectedly .

Ten days after the theft, Myo Min Aye, wife of Ko Tin Min, our boat manager,

經過這件不幸的事件後，我們繼續航行，旅行，最後飛到茵萊湖快快的視察我們在那兒的項目。警察跟我們說要破案跟找回失物的機會很小，但是，事情的發展出人意料之外。

被小偷光顧十天後，*Myo Min Aye*，她是船經理 *Ko Tin Min* 的老婆，試著打到老公失竊的手機。神奇的電話響了，居然有人接起電話。對話很快的變成談判，*Ko Tin Min* 假裝是 *Myo Min Aye* 的哥哥，繼續與對方交涉。顯然小偷們在緬甸北部找不到 *iPhone 6*，*iPad*，*Kindle*，還有其他高端設備的買家，更不要說是硬碟了。

來回談判，用美金一千元可以買回我們所有失竊的東西。對我們來說是划算的，對小偷們來說也算是個好價錢。價錢談好後，*Ko Tin Min* 打給他真的姊夫，他認識警察總部的高層。很快地，來自曼德勒跟實皆兩個分局的員警，都動員起來了。

相約好的這天，四月四日，*Ko Tin Min* 捆好一大疊的緬甸幣，前往指定的地方準備進行交易，地點在依洛瓦底江畔。小偷們不知道這一大捆錢只有最上面跟最下面的幾張是五千緬元，裡面全部是一千面額的鈔票。

警察建議 *Ko Tin Min* 帶一個伴前去，意思是帶一個保鏢。

tried calling her husband's lost phone. Miraculously the phone rang and someone picked up the phone. Soon conversations turned to negotiations as Ko Tin Min pretended to be Myo Min Aye's brother and took over the discussions. Apparently, the thieves could not find ready buyers for the iPhone 6, iPad, Kindle and other high end kit in upper Myanmar, let alone the hard drives.

Through back and forth negotiations, a price was fixed for the return of the items - USD1000. That would seem a bargain for us and a good price and prize for the thieves. Once an agreement was struck, however, Ko Tin Min contacted his real brother-in-law who knew some big wigs within the divisional police headquarters. Soon police from two divisions, Mandalay and Sagaing were mobilized.

On the assigned day, April 4, Ko Tin Min bundled up a large stack of Burmese money in Kyats and headed to a pre-arranged site along the bank of the Irrawaddy River where the transaction was supposed to take place. What the thieves did not know was that the top and bottom few bills were 5000 Kyat denomination, but all of the interior stack was smaller notes in 1000 Kyats.

The police suggested that he should go with a "partner", a bodyguard of sorts. This middle age guy was called by the pseudonym Mr. X (apologies to our filmmaker Xavier, who is also known as X). He had a crucifix tattooed on his chest and always made sure that his shirt buttons were open to show it. He was

said to have murdered several people, maybe five or six, but had since reformed himself and now served as a police informer. For a USD30 fee, he seemed like a "good" guy to have around when dealing with thieves or thugs! The pair, Ko Tin Min and the body guard, would go rendezvous with the devils.

The police were more civilized in their attire and arrived separately, over thirty of them. Two were dressed as monks, with even their heads shaved. One policeman and one policewoman acted as lovers, dating nearby on the bank. One was dressed as a fisherman with a basket; inside were handcuffs and his gun. The rest were hiding nearby waiting for action.

My team and I waited anxiously on our boat. It turned out to take several hours, which felt at times like years. At the assigned time, the thieves called and delayed, changing the timing to later. Everyone continued to wait.

Finally, at around 4pm, a small motorized boat pulled up to the bank and four young people, three men and one woman, got out of the boat and walked up to Ko Tin Min and his "partner" who were waiting at the bank. Just as the transaction was beginning, the police swooped in for their kill. One thug, particularly alert, struggled and got away, running for his life. Three others were immediately apprehended.

The operation was a success, despite the man who got away, who turned out to

這位中年男子的化名叫 Mr. X〈在這跟我們的製片 Xavier 說聲抱歉，他也叫 X〉。Mr. X 胸口有個十字架的刺青，襯衫上面的釦子總是會解開，確定刺青是可以被展示到。聽說他殺過好幾個人，好像五、六個，但是後來從良，現在是警察的線民。以三十塊美金來說，他看起來算是夠「好」到去跟小偷或是土匪交涉的人選。Ko Tin Min 跟保鑣就這樣前去與惡魔赴約。

穿著制服的警察看起來很文明，他們分批到達，一共有三十位。兩位喬裝成和尚，他們甚至把頭髮都剃掉；一位男警跟女警假裝是一對戀人，在河畔談戀愛；一位員警喬裝成漁夫還帶著竹簍，竹簍裡裝的是手銬還有他的槍；其他員警分別在附近伺機而動。

我跟我的團隊在船上很緊張，搞了好幾個鐘頭，但是感覺好像是好幾年。約定的時間到了，小偷們打來說要延後時間，大家只好繼續等候。

終於差不多在四點，一艘配有馬達的小船靠岸，隨同四個年輕人，三個男生跟一個女生，走向在岸上的 Ko Tin Min 跟他的保鑣。當交易正要開始進行時，一群警察衝去逮人，一個土匪很敏捷，奮力掙脫，被他逃掉了，但是剩下的全部被逮捕。

be the ringleader of this gang. The woman, turned out to be the leader's wife. Before long, she and the others led the police back to their home, a makeshift bamboo shed on the bank of the river where many families, especially fishermen and bamboo rafts men, make their temporary home six months of the year when the water is low.

There the police found much more loot; radios, phones, electrical appliances, knickknacks, and even a bolt cutter and sharp long knives. They even had a battery and electric wiring for illegal electro-fishing. And another surprise, the woman had two young children living in their den. As the police noted, this gang had been operating along the riverbank of Mandalay for a while. It was one of two such gangs; the other is larger in scale and still at large. Perhaps they will become our next catch.

Ko Tin Min identified and retrieved his phone. Camilla got back her phone and, thank goodness, her hard drive. Her Kindle and all the items that Berry lost were still unaccounted for. Obviously the gang wanted to trick us again, as they only brought a small part of their loot to trade with us. We were glad that we solicited the help of the police.

While we are now all scattered to our various work sites, we still await another call, though not with so much anxiety. This time, hopefully, it will be from the police, letting us know that all the remaining items have been found.

這個行動很成功，儘管有一個人逃脫，他恰好是這個集團的首領。那位女生剛好是首領的老婆。隨後，她跟其他人帶著警察到他們的家，那是靠岸臨時搭建的竹編屋，附近聚集了很多個家庭，很多漁夫跟划竹筏的船夫，在枯水期的那六個月裡會住在這裡。

在他們家裡，警察發現許多贓物，無線電、電器用品、家飾品，還有斷線鉗跟一把鋒利的長刀，甚至還有電魚的電池跟電線。更令人意外的發現，這名女子帶著兩個小孩跟這群人住在一起。根據警察的筆錄，這群人在曼德勒的河岸犯罪已經有一段時間。在這裡的犯罪集團還有另一個，另一個更大，尚未被逮捕歸案。也許下一次換他們被捕。

Ko Tin Min 找回他的電話。*Camilla* 找回她的電話，還好也找回她的硬碟。但是她的 *Kindle* 跟 *Berry* 失竊的東西還是沒有回來。結果，我們又被小偷騙了，土匪只交回我們一小部分失竊的東西，不是原本談好的條件。但很慶幸我們找了警察幫忙。

現在我們每個人都在不同的地方進行我們各自的工作，我們也還在等電話響起，那是一種不安的期待。希望下通電話是警察打來的，打來告訴我們失竊的東西全部找回。

BLUE SKY, WHITE PEAKS AND GREEN HILLS

藍天，白峰，綠山丘

Paro, Bhutan – April 24, 2015

藍天，白峰，綠山丘 **晉見不丹國王陛下皇太后的母親**

「這是一個非常吉祥的徵兆！」*Neten* 喇嘛帶著微笑說。我們終於打破沉默了，昨晚是我第一次見到他，在山下的房子中，他看起來莊嚴，嚴肅。

雖然只有四十九歲，他的舉止像個年長的老師。畢竟他是這個一百二十人寺院的院長，寺裡大部分都是年輕男孩。他們住在嘎灑宗一棟很大的城堡裡，嘎灑宗是不丹二十個行政和司法管轄區裡最北，最大也是最高的一個區域。他另外也掌管二十間附屬寺院，大多座落在令人頭暈的高原，靠近西藏。

嘎灑宗這棟建築物是眾多建築裡最老的一棟，建於十七世紀中，很壯觀；四周被森林圍繞，雄偉的雪山在後面襯著，這棟城堡就好像從森林裡竄出。我會選擇來嘎撒是因為幾天前在曼谷時我研究衛星影像顯示，在喜瑪拉雅山的南向坡有很豐富的冰河，應該可以看得到犛牛群漫遊在夏天高原牧場上。我馬上改變行程，降落到不丹後直接前往嘎撒。

BLUE SKY, WHITE PEAKS AND GREEN HILLS

And audience with Her Majesty the Royal Grandmother of Bhutan

"That is a very auspicious sign," said Lama Neten with a sliver of smile, finally. It seemed at last we had broken the ice as he looked very serious and solemn when I first met him the night before, at a home down the hill.

Though only 49 years of age, his demeanor was like that of an old teacher. After all, he is the abbot of a monastery with 120 monks, most of them boys. And they reside in this monumental castle of Gasa Dzong, the seat of one of the twenty Dzongkhags (Districts) of Bhutan and the northernmost, largest and highest of all the Districts. Below him, but above him in elevation, he controls another twenty smaller sub-monasteries, most sitting at dizzying height of the plateau bordering Tibet.

The architecture of Gasa Dzong, one of the oldest of the Dzongs dates from the mid 17th Century, with an impressive edifice rising above the surrounding forest at a spur, with a majestic snow range as backdrop. It looks out to yet another range of snow peaks, one of which rose like a monument of ice sculpture. I chose to come to Gasa based on a study of the satellite images just

當我到達寺院時，我告訴 *Neten* 喇嘛，剛剛在來路上遇見三隻公鹿，牠們走到路的兩旁好像是為我開道一樣。我還拍到一張照片，一隻角很大的公鹿躲在樹後面看著我。*Neten* 喇嘛很訝異，他說鹿通常只有在晚上才看得到，白天幾乎看不到牠們的身影。

透過我們的翻譯響導 *Yeshi*（他是位狂熱的觀鳥家），喇嘛把我的遭遇跟一個佛教故事做相比，關於一位西藏的聖人 *Milarepa*。故事是這樣的，*Milarepa* 在禪修時有一隻被獵人和獵狗追殺的鹿躲到 *Milarepa* 背後，他為了救鹿於是設法安撫獵人與狗，最終那隻受驚的鹿獲得了解救，於是這成了藏傳佛教裡經常被傳誦的故事。

也許 *Neten* 喇嘛真的很相信徵兆。我們的談話很愉快，儘管他隨後就要去接嘎灑區的州長，很少去寺院的領導今天要打算去寺院拜訪。分手前，我答應會幫忙寺院一棟才動工的建築物，這棟房舍將會用來做和尚的學校還有給附近幼齡的小孩學英文。

政府會提供建築物的建造費，但不包括內裝跟設備。*Neten* 喇嘛為了籌錢來完成這個項目而奔波，足跡踏遍整個區域。我答應幫他找一位贊助者，信佛的，必需的話 *CERS* 也會捐款。以規模大小來說，這項目不會太困難，做得來，它是個展現我們善意的好機會，為我們的將來鋪

a few days ago when I was in Bangkok. The images showed that the area has an abundance of glaciers on the southern slope of the Himalayas, with high pastures among which I could expect to find yak herders roaming. I changed my entire itinerary of travels overnight, and landed in Bhutan heading straight to Gasa.

As I arrived at the monastery, I recounted to Lama Neten that I ran into three stag deers on my approach to the monastery, running off to two sides of the road as if making way for me. I even captured in pictures one of the deer, a huge stag with a set of large anthers, looking at me from behind the trees. Lama Neten seemed surprised by my account, and mentioned that they usually only see the deer at night, almost never during day time.

Through Yeshi, our guide/interpreter who is an avid birdwatcher, the Lama related my encounter to a Buddhist story of the Tibetan saint Milarepa. While in meditative retreat, Milarepa was approached by a frightened stag deer being chased by a hunter and his dog. He managed to pacify both the dog and the hunter with compassion, and the deer was saved. This episode became an often-told story within Tibetan Buddhism.

Perhaps Lama Neten really believed in the omen of my visit. We had a great and warm chat thereafter, despite that soon he had to rush off to receive the Governor of Gasa District, making one of his rare visits to the monastery. But

Gasa Dzong with mountain in background / 群山環繞的嘎灑宗

before we parted ways, I agreed to help the monastery with a new building that just started construction. Its purpose is to house a new school for the monks and lay children of the area, learning English at an early age.

The government has provided the building costs, but nothing for the interior furnishing or equipment. Lama Neten had been most busy, traveling throughout his District in order to raise the money needed to complete the project. I promised to find him a Buddhist patron among my friends, as well as providing matching fund from CERS if necessary. In scale, the project is not too ambitious and quite modest, and it would pave the way with good will for many exciting projects I wanted to start in the surrounding area.

A road was just completed to the Dzong two years ago. Prior to that, it might have taken several days of trekking or on horseback to reach here. These days, the famous hot spring down by the river is visited everyday by Bhutanese from far and wide. Many cross the entire country, riding in cars on rough roads for two days to reach this famous medicinal spring enclave.

Five bath houses sit next to the river, including a walled and gated one for the Royal family. I took a dip with all the locals, together with many of the elderly ladies baring their tops. It seemed most natural, in a country where nature still reigns. Matching all the hype about Bhutan's Gross National Happiness, everyone seemed particularly contented, especially

路，有好多令我興奮的項目要在這附近進行。

通往 Dzong 的路兩年前才鋪好，以前可是花上好幾天的
徒步加上騎馬才到得了。現在，有個靠河的溫泉出了名，
每天都有來自不同地方的不丹人來泡。有些人開了兩天崎
嶇的車橫跨不丹，就為了來到這個有醫療效果的溫泉。

河流旁有五間溫泉屋，包括一間有著外牆和大門的皇室御
用溫泉屋。我跟當地人一起泡，其中許多老婦人是赤裸上
身的。這再自然不過了，尤其在這個自然為王的國度裡。
依照不丹聞名的國民幸福指數來看，每個人似乎都很滿
足，特別是泡在溫泉裡的時候。

這裡真的很能感受到平靜，可以很放鬆。我們的司機
Shacha 非常的有禮貌，車子開的很慢很小心，連在柏油
路上也是。每當他發現我們把相機拿出來的時候，他就會
把車子停下來。一度，一頭驚慌的小牛，跟牠的牛群走失
了，Shacha 還把車子停下來，走出車外，試圖把小牛趕
回到媽媽那裡。

我們在一個清澈的山泉溪旁野餐，白色的杜鵑正全然盛
開。Yeshi 跟 Shacha 靜靜的跟我們一起用餐，為了表示對
我們的尊敬，他們的謙卑讓我們有點不好意思。我們一起
分享的菜他們也不太碰，兩個人各吃了兩盤赤米飯加一點

while soaking in the hot spring.

Indeed my experience here had been most calm and relaxed. Our driver Shacha was extremely polite, driving slowly and carefully, even when we were on paved roads. Whenever he noticed us raising the camera, he would stop the car. At one point when a calf was frightened and parted with the herd, Shacha stopped his car, got out, and tried to usher the calf back to the mother.

We had one picnic lunch together by a clear mountain stream rushing by, with the white rhododendron in full bloom. Both Yeshi and Shacha ate quietly with us, showing utmost respect and modesty which made us a bit uncomfortable. They barely touched the dishes we shared, and ate two plates of plain red rice each, with simple spicy curried sauce over it.

簡單的咖哩醬淋在上面。

我對不丹高原的迷戀，成為我關注這裏的焦點，它的植物、動物跟氂牛也是很值得被研究的，但是這些必須待我們在當地建立多些關係時才能執行。我個人是對氂牛牧民的文化很感興趣，尤其是他們近年來受到冬蟲夏草價錢高漲的影響，因此將傳統的乳品製作放到一旁。昂貴的高原蟲草在中國跟亞洲很受歡迎，因為人們相信它有療效。我想知道，這個歷史久遠的遊牧民族價值裡，經濟面、文化面和精神面所受到的衝擊和影響是什麼。

這趟的旅行算是為未來的旅程探路，建立一些關係好讓我們近期可以在這裡進行跨學科的項目。一個比我預期更早的項目可能實現。

就在嘎灑宗下方的小村莊只有五戶人家，我在其中一戶人家裡吃晚餐。*Bago* 的房子已經有六十五年歷史了，快要被拆掉，好蓋新的房子。*Bago* 的身分證上的出生日是一九四二年一月一日。但是他認為他其實應該出生的更早，但是那個年代有誰在記錄生日呢。我們希望可以說服這家人把這棟這麼棒的傳統房子留下來，未來可以當成我們進入高原的基地。破舊的木牆、階梯好像都在跟我們訴說過往的點點滴滴。它看出去的景緻非常漂亮，嘎灑宗城堡在後面昇起，遠處有白雪覆蓋的山峰，下面

While my focus in Bhutan is fixated on the high plateau, its flora, fauna and yak herders, it has to wait until we can build up enough local contacts to execute such projects. My personal interest relates to the yak herders' culture, which in recent years has been much affected by the meteoric rise in prices of Cordyceps, a high altitude caterpillar fungus believed to have medicinal value for Chinese and Asians alike. Even the traditional means of dairy production has been sidelined, with it much of the age-old nomadic values, both in economic, cultural and spiritual terms.

This trip can be considered a reconnaissance for future trips to come, establishing some connections so that we can initiate multiple projects in the near future, covering a diverse range of disciplines. One such project may manifest itself sooner than I expected.

Just below the Dzong monastery of Gasa, I had dinner at a home in a small village with only five households. The house of Bago is sixty-five years old, soon to be torn down to make way for a new house the family wants to build. Bago's own age was listed on his ID card with birthdate as January 1, 1942. He thought he is older, though in those days, no one really recorded their birth date. We wanted to convince the family to preserve this wonderful traditional house, hopefully to be used as a future base of our operation into the high plateau. The worn wood, walls, ladders and all were like whispers from the past, telling tales of a time gone by. It also looks out to a most beautiful

Old house with Dzong in background / 嘎灑宗腳下的舊房子

scenery, with the Dzong castle rising behind, the snow range and peaks in a distance, and green hills and valleys below.

The family even has in their chapel, one of the most important relics of Bhutan. One shoe, in red and with embroidered shell, was bestowed on ancestors of Bago's wife, by Ngawang Namgyel, the first Zhabdrung Rinpoche who came to Bhutan in 1616AD when he was exiled from Tibet. He was considered the founder of Bhutan. With luck and blessing, we hope to save this particular house from demolition, and maintain it into the future with some useful and positive role.

As if the encounter with the stag deer was not enough of a good omen, while driving back to the capital of Thimphu on the same morning, I ran into a beautiful bright green snake of over two meters in length. Just moments later, two Assamese Macaque monkeys crossed the road in front of us. As we descended down

是翠綠的丘陵和山谷。

這戶人家的家裡甚至有個小經堂，珍藏不丹很重要的文化遺產。一隻紅色的鞋子，繡著貝殼，由阿旺·南嘉（Ngawang Namgyel），第一位夏仲活佛所贈與給 Bago 老婆的祖先的。活佛在 1616 年從西藏流亡到不丹，他被視為是建立不丹的人。帶著運氣與賜福，我們希望可以搶救這棟房子，維護它，讓它未來可以發揮正面有意義的功用。

好像遇到公鹿還不夠幸運，在我們回到首都廷布的路上，我還遇見一條鮮綠色的蛇，超過兩米長；過一會兒，兩隻阿薩姆獼猴從我們面前走過，這都發生在同一天的早上。當我們往海拔低的方向下降到 Phojikja，還沒到普納卡前 (punakha Dzong 這裡有非常令人驚豔的城堡)，我看到一種非常非常稀有的鳥：白腹鷺。這種鳥在不丹可能剩不到三十隻，是瀕臨絕種的鳥類，估計在地球上只剩不到兩百隻。我的相機在遠距抓到牠的輪廓，這是我這趟旅程的縮影，也是最滿足的一刻。我的腦袋隨著沒鋪柏油的道路左右搖晃，此刻的我終於適應這裡了，不管是環境還是文化。

幸運的事再來一樁，不丹國女王陛下皇太后的母親在廷布接見了我。八十五歲的她是世界上唯一的皇家祖母。

to Phojikha, before reaching Punakha Dzong with a most impressive castle, I spotted the rarest of birds, the White-bellied Heron. There may be less than thirty birds remaining in all of Bhutan. It is also one of the most endangered birds in the world with perhaps less than two hundred birds worldwide. Capturing it with my camera, though like a silhouette at a distance, was the epitome and most satisfying moment of the entire trip. By now, I have caught on even culturally, having my head shaking from side to side, as we rode through bumps and hitches over the unpaved road.

Topping all these, however, was during my final day in Thimphu, I had an audience with Her Majesty the Royal Grandmother. At 85 years of age, she is the only Royal Grandmother in the world. We met six years ago when I first visited Bhutan in 2009, accompanying her on a yearly religious offering journey to some of the most important monasteries, making blessing for the Royal Family and the people of Bhutan.

On this day, however, our meeting was in her beautiful Royal Palace, up on the hill above Thimphu. Joining us at the meeting was her 91-years-old sister Tashi, and her nephew Dasho Benji, an older gentleman who is a most knowledgeable naturalist and has been crucial in establishing many of Bhutan's environmental and nature protection policies. Benji's multiple portfolio included serving as the country's Chief Justice in the 1980s.

我們第一次見面是在六年前，我第一次拜訪不丹，我陪她去了具有宗教性質的奉獻之旅，去了一些很重要的寺廟，她祈求賜福與皇家和不丹的人民。

這天我們的聚會是在她那美麗的皇宮裡，在廷布的山丘上。與會的還有她九十一歲的姐姐 Tashi，和姪子 Dasho Benji。Dasho Benji 是位年長的紳士，也是知識豐富的自然博物學者，對不丹的環境與自然保護政策扮演很重要的角色。Benji 也曾經在一九八零年代擔任不丹的首席大法官。

我跟皇太后的母親和她的姊姊聊的很愉快，她們兩位都是錫金的公主，一邊聊天一邊配著茶跟精緻的手工點心。兩位姊妹不時回憶起年輕時的日子，在葛倫堡時，她們的父親曾經接待過多位要前往拉薩的探險家。鼎鼎有名的亞歷山大‧大衛‧尼爾也曾是座上賓；還有姊妹們最喜歡的約瑟夫‧洛克博士，她們說了許多關於他的事。洛克博士是我在國家地理雜誌的前輩，在一九二零年到一九四零年間貢獻很多故事給雜誌社。我答應皇太后的母親會把我收藏的約瑟夫‧洛克博士的書寄給她。

皇室接待的貴賓還包括十三世達賴喇嘛，當他自西藏開始流亡，曾在不丹待了半年。為了表達謝意，達賴送給皇室一件非常罕見的唐卡，到現在還是由皇太后的母親保管。

Royal Grandmother, sister Tashi and Benji / 皇太后的母親（右二），姊姊 Tashi，姪子 Benji（左一）

With the Royal Grand Mother and her sister, both Princesses of Sikkim, we had a wonderful discussion, over tea and some delicately home-made snack. The two sisters reminisced their younger days. In Kalimpong, their father entertained many early explorers on their way to Lhasa in Tibet. Besides big names like Alexandra David-Neel, one particular gentleman the aging sisters are most fond of and talked about at length was Dr Joseph Rock, my predecessor at the National Geographic who contributed many stories to the magazine between the 1920s to the 40s. I promised to send to the Royal Grandmother books on Dr Rock that I have in my library.

Select guests of their family included, for six months, the 13th Dalai Lama

Punakha Dzong castle / 普納卡城堡

隨後，皇太后母親的孫女 Ashi Kesang Choeden Wangchuk 公主讓我見識這件珍品。這位公主是皇太后母親最疼愛的，所以她的名字跟祖母一樣。她也是現任國王的堂妹，有時被稱為 Baby Kesang。她現在負責唐卡修復中心，裡面工作人員全是不丹的和尚，她將所有的時間與精力都花在這件非常重要的任務上。

皇太后母親柔嫩的手握著我的手，我們聊了許多她鍾愛的話題。她是在葛倫堡耶穌會的聖若瑟修院和英國受的教育。嫁給不丹的三世國王後，她將重心放在國內所有的寺廟，確定他們有足夠的資金跟支援，可以將許多宗教聖地修復，以回到其昔日的輝煌。她最近從事的工作具有極大的意義，將蓮花生大師的壁畫與唐卡持續出版，祂是西藏佛教，寧瑪傳承——紅教的始祖。

when he was in exile from Tibet. As a token of appreciation, the family was given a rare Thangka by his Holiness, which today is in the possession of the Royal Grandmother. I was later shown this rare piece of art by Princess Ashi Kesang Choeden Wangchuk, a favorite granddaughter of the Royal Grandmother, notable through bearing exactly the same name as her grandmother. She is also a cousin of the current King. Sometimes known as the Baby Kesang, she is now in charge of the Thangka Restoration Center, staffed by monks of Bhutan, and devotes her entire time and energy to this very important undertaking.

With her soft and tender hand holding mine, the Royal Grandmother and I chatted over many subjects endearing to her heart. Educated by Jesuits of the St Joseph Convent at Kalimpong, she later studied in the UK. After marrying the Third King of Bhutan, she has been a wonderful patron to all the monasteries of the country, making sure that they receive adequate funding and support, including restoring many religious sites to their former glory. Her latest project is of monumental proportion, supporting over the years publication of the murals and Thangkas on Guru Rinpoche (Padmasambhava), founder of the Nyingma lineage of Tibetan Buddhism.

As a parting gift, Her Majesty signed for me, with golden ink, that very important religious volume on Guru Rinpoche, as best wishes to my future

Princess Kesang restoring 13th Dalai's gift Thangka /
與 Kesang 公主觀賞正在修復的唐卡（十三世達賴所贈送）

道別時，皇太后母親特別用金色的墨水為我簽名，這本關於蓮花生大師非常重要的書，祝福我未來在她深愛的不丹一切順利。我向她請求，希望她可以賜福與我們，就像小孩子需要被賜福，讓他長大可以掌控自己的人生。我特別告訴她，這本重要的書不會成為咖啡桌上的飾品，這一件具有精神意義的文物，會被我放在香港家中最莊嚴的地方，敬拜堂。

今天早晨下了春雨，高山都被覆蓋上了剛下的雪。希望幾個月後我回到這裡時，天空是藍的，山峰是白的，山丘是翠綠的。

endeavor in her beloved country. I asked for Her Majesty's Royal blessing to our projects, just as a small child would need blessing, until he gets older and take on a life of his own. I noted to her that this important work is not a coffee table book, but an object of spiritual dimension that would take up a place of honor in the private chapel at my home in Hong Kong.

This morning, we had a sprinkle of spring shower, and the high mountains were clothed in a shade of fresh snow. In a few months I hope to return, when the sky is blue, the peaks are white, and the hills are green.

Gasa's blue sky white peak and green hills / 嘎灑的藍天白峰綠山丘

探索湄公河與支流

MEKONG AND TRIBUTARY EXPLORATION

Luang Namtha, Laos – July 30, 2015

瑯南塔　寮國　二零一五年七月三十日

探索湄公河與支流

突然間，回憶帶我回到了小時候，大概五、六歲的那時，我把家中的沙發當作船，前後左右晃動，想像我正在一艘小船上經過湍急的河流。六十幾年後的今天，我在現實裡真正體驗這樣的事，只不過天氣沒有我想像中的那樣好。

雨很大，熱帶暴風雨下個不停，無處可躲。但，為什麼要躲呢？我很享受這場雨，雨將夏日中午的氣溫降到一個比較可以忍受的溫度。我只有一塊塑膠布遮蓋，畢博士坐在我旁邊，很欣然地接受。畢竟他是個自然主義者，身為田野科學家應該享受這環境、氣候和動物，一切大自然給予地球的。甚至是在這裡活躍的水蛭。

還好畢博士穿著一件防水的夾克，夾克很自然地成為防水衣蓋住腰包，包裡面放著相機、望遠鏡、筆記本，可能還有一些有的沒有的東西。雨可能還會下好一陣子，可能幾小時，我們得趕快用竹子搭個臨時遮雨棚，要不然我那些堆得高高的行李跟背包都會濕透。

064　探索湄公河與支流

MEKONG AND TRIBUTARY EXPLORATION

Suddenly my memory went way back, to a time when I was a little child, maybe five or six years old. I used to rock myself in the sofa at home, forward and backward and from side to side, imagining that I was in a tiny boat, going through rough torrents on a river. Here I was, going through it in reality, some sixty years later. But the weather wasn't as nice as I had imagined.

Heavy rain was pouring down, a non-stop tropical storm. And I had nowhere to hide. But then, why hide? I was thoroughly enjoying this rain. It took the summer heat down to a far more bearable temperature even during midday. I only had a plastic tarp to cover myself. Bill Bleisch, sitting next to me, also took it quite naturally. He is a naturalist after all, a field scientist who should enjoy the environment, the weather, the animals and all that nature bestows on this earth. Maybe even the leeches that thrive in such a climate!

Bill, however, had a waterproof jacket over him, and casually pulled up his tarp to cover his oversized fanny pack that had all his camera gear, binoculars, notebooks, and probably a large sundry of other knick-knacks. The rain would last for a long time, a good few hours, until all our luggage and backpacks piled

我們處於這趟探險的最後一站，研究湄公河離開中國進入泰國跟寮國的邊境的這一小段，也是它快要往下進入寮國舊城龍坡邦前。五天的湄公河航行後，我們到了琅南塔，這裡有個湄公河的主要支流。我突然有個很棒的想法，把所有人，一共十二個人換到兩艘小船上，用兩天的時間回到上游，我們停車的那個地方。

直到目前為止，我們坐的船還算舒服，*120* 呎的瘦長型船，白天它是我們的家。船上有八個可以坐的套座，兩間廁所跟一個吧檯。我們帶來的零食把桌子堆得滿滿的。現在，我們要換到兩艘不到 *20* 呎長，沒有頂篷的船，每艘只能載六個人。這樣的決定究竟是聰明的還是愚蠢的實在有待商榷，不過這也視乎每個人是怎麼看待探險家的生活方式。

對我來說這不只是生活方式，這就是我的生活。但是對我一些同事來說，當初會參與，是因為這是份令人興奮的工作；而冒險總會有不如意的時候，就像現在的暴風雨。頓時我想到世上的一群船上人家，他們必須離開自己的家，搭著小船去尋求生存的機會，我很同情那些難民。想想我們有多幸運，我們各自的船上旅行有著不同的目的，不同的命運。

琅南塔，寮國最北邊的省，鄰近中國，*CERS* 已經在這裡

high under a make-shift bamboo canopy would all become wet.

We were on the last leg of an exploration trip to study the Mekong where it left China and became the border between Thailand and Laos for a short stretch before flowing further down to the old capital of Laos at Luang Prabang. After five days on the Mekong, at the confluence of the Namtha, a major tributary at this section of the Mekong, I had the great idea of transferring ourselves, a team of twelve, to two tiny riverboats in order to return to Luang Namtha two days upstream where our cars were parked.

Up till now we had been on a rather comfortable long and narrow boat of 120 foot length, effectively our day-time home. It came with eight booths for sitting, and was equipped with both a toilet, and a bar! And we set out an entire tableful of junk food we brought along. But the move to the two open-top boats, barely 20 feet in length, each taking six of us sitting in pairs, was debatably wise or stupid, depending on the attitude each of us held in embracing an explorer's lifestyle.

For me, it was not just a lifestyle, but my life. But for some of my colleagues, who took this up as an exciting job, adventures can at times turn sour, like at this moment in the midst of a torrential rain. Momentarily my thoughts went out to another type of boat people, those who had to leave their homes in tiny boats in search of basic survival and security. My sympathy went to the

Boat landing below lodge / 旅館下方停靠的船隻

many refugees throughout the world. How fortunate we were that our trip was for a different purpose, and with a different destiny.

CERS has been involved in Luang Namtha, a northernmost province of Laos bordering China, for over three years. Our goal here is to better understand the wildlife, including large mammals like wild elephants, in a large protected area which included many farming communities within its boundaries. Bill is also interested in the very active wildlife trading, legal or illegal, crossing the border into China.

My current trip is in the hope of integrating some cultural aspects into our project, given that there are several ethnic groups living in the vicinity. The Khmu, Akha, Mien, Lanten and Hmong people all make the area their homes. With the jungle all around us, traveling by water was one way to reach outlying villages. Deang Souliya, one of CERS' two local staffs, is Khmu. The boat we chartered would take us also past his home, right on the edge of the Mekong.

At Houay Xai, we stayed a night at the posh-looking but rather economical Phonevichit Hotel overlooking the

三年了。我們的目的是了解這裡的野生動物，特別針對大型的哺乳動物，像是野生大象。這裡有一個很大的保護區，裡面也有幾個務農的社區。畢博士對於野生動物的交易非常有興趣，不管入境到中國的方式是合法還是非法的。

我這一趟去是希望能夠將當地的文化融入在我們的項目裡，因為這附近住著好幾個民族。像是克木族、阿卡人、緬族、*Lanten* 還有苗族都把這裡當家。四處都是叢林，到這些偏遠村落的方式要走水路。*Deang Souliya* 是 CERS 當地的員工，他是克木族人。我們包下的船會帶我們經過他的家，就在湄公河畔。

我們在會曬（*Houay Xai*）待了一晚，住進看起來豪華但是價錢實惠的濱江大酒店（*Phonevichit*），可以俯瞰湄公河。在湄公河的第一晚我坐在陽台上欣賞著幾隻壁虎，牠們趴在燈上，演出即興狂想曲，一隻隻被燈光吸引過來的蚊子跟小蟲，全部被壁虎捕獲。靜靜的，我感謝上帝創造飛的比蒼蠅還慢的蚊子，讓我們偶爾也有機會可以復仇。

我們在會曬上船，很多遊客會在這個小鎮搭船，然後花上兩天的時間遊湄公河。旅途的另一個終點在龍坡邦。現在正是暑假旺季，一些小船會載超過五十位的外國學生，由老師帶他們去遠足。也有一些船會載著背包客跟當地人在

Mekong. That first night along the Mekong, I sat back on the balcony and rejoiced at the silhouettes of several geckos perching on the lamp, performing a rhapsody in snapping up mosquitoes and bugs attracted to the light. Quietly, I thanked god for creating mosquitoes which fly slower than flies. So occasionally we too could avenge our miseries.

We boarded our long boat at Houay Xai, a small town where many tourists embark for a two-day river trip along the Mekong. The other end of this journey would be Luang Prabang. As this was during the height of the summer holidays, some long boats would be packing over fifty foreign students in a single boat, led by teachers on summer excursion trips. Other boats would have groups of backpackers among a few locals traveling up and down the river.

Deang's home was in the small village of Houay Sor, perched right above the north bank of the Mekong. As we disembarked and started hiking up the bank, a tractor came roaring up the gulley following a track partly washed away by the rain. It was hauling rocks retrieved from the riverbed; foundation stone for a new building. As the incline was steep, half a dozen women were pushing the tractor up the hill. It seemed quite common to see women in the countryside doing the hardest job, while the men take up the easier part of steering, as in this case with the tractor.

河流上下行走。

Deang 的家在 Houay Sor 的一個小村莊，坐落在湄公河的北岸。當我們正準備下船上岸時，看見一台拖拉機正從溝裡把另一台被大雨沖走的卡車拉上來。他們準備把石頭從河床拖上來，好當作新的建築物的地基。由於斜坡很陡，需要六個女人推著拖拉機往上走。在這裡似乎很常看到婦女負責粗重的工作，男生做輕鬆的，像是掌握拖拉機的方向盤。

還沒抵達村莊前，我們得先經過一個竹編的大門。竹子的一端被削的尖銳，像矛一樣。大門應該是用來抵擋惡魔跟敵人的，但尖銳的那端卻往內彎。

Deang 正在為他的父母親蓋新房，水泥磚塊取代竹編牆，錫屋頂取代茅草頂。這樣的屋子被視為是財富與現代的象徵。冰箱被放在家裡最重要的位置，正對門口。冰箱是個禮物，想必是 Deang 未婚妻的嫁妝。他們計畫在 2016 年結婚。村民們圍著房子想好好的看看這些奇怪的訪客。一些克木族年長的婦女臉上跟身體都留有刺青。

下一站到白崩過夜。Karim 經營的全新民宿有十二個房間，並可俯瞰湄公河，就在我們停船的旁邊。這裡大多數的民宿都是那種只供床跟早餐的。Karim 的 Mekong

Baby in Laos / 寮國的嬰兒

Before reaching the village, we passed through a gate made from bamboo. One end of these bamboos was shaven sharp, like spears. With all sharp edges facing inward, the gate was believed to ward off evils and enemies alike.

Deang was in the process of building a new house for his parents, with cement bricks rather than bamboo walls and tin roof rather than thatched. Such houses were considered a sign of wealth and modernity. A refrigerator held the place of honor in the middle of the wall, facing the entrance. This was a gift, presumably part of a dowry, from Deang's fiancé. They expect to be married in 2016. Villagers gathered around the house to have a good look at the strange looking visitors. Some older Khmu ladies still sported tattoos on their faces and bodies.

Riverside Lodge 是最貴的，一晚要價三十五塊美金，但是也是最進步、景色最好，並帶有靠河岸的陽台，腳下就是湄公河。我們選了景色最好的房間。

對街有一家餐廳，掛著印度的國旗，打著正宗印度料理的招牌。結果 *Karim* 也是這餐廳的老闆。然而 *Karim* 是從孟加拉來的。他不但是老闆也是廚師。隔天早餐，一向笑咪咪的 *Karim* 穿著一件花襯衫跟圍裙，在廚房裡為我們準備餐點。像這種什麼事都親力親為的經營模式在偏遠地區是很常見的。

這裡的湄公河跟伊洛瓦底江往西的緬甸很不一樣。湄公河中段有比較多的石灰岩山丘，潔淨天然，有很多綠色叢林，但是畢博士很快的指出這些不是原始森林而是次森林。我們幾乎看不到任何鳥類，或是聽到蟋蟀那類的昆蟲在夜裡鳴叫。湄公河裡的魚也很稀少，儘管我們買到一尾身長快到一公尺、並且五公斤重的鯰魚。我也只看到大象兩次。

這裡的村民不像住在依洛瓦底江的那些會在河裡洗澡或是洗衣服。河上運行的船不多，有些當地的擺渡以及捕魚的小舢舨。河道不寬，河岸可以耕種的地方很小。作物大部分都種在山坡上，輪番種植玉米、豆子、糯米，收割完後燒田翻土，準備種另一種作物。我沒有看到水壩，但是在

Our next stop was Pak Beng for the night. Karim ran a brand new lodge with twelve rooms overlooking the Mekong, next to the boat landing. Most other lodgings in this small village seemed to be home-stay Bed & Breakfast type affairs. Karim's Mekong Riverside Lodge was the most pricy; at USD $35 per night, but it seemed the most sophisticated, hugging the river bank with balconies looking down to the Mekong. We took up the rooms with the best views.

Across the street was a restaurant with a sign outside sporting an Indian flag advertising authentic Indian cuisine. It turned out Karim also owned the Indian restaurant. Yet Karim is from Bangladesh. Not only did he own the restaurant, he was also the chef. At breakfast the following morning, an always-smiling Karim was seen in a most colorful shirt, donning his apron and in the kitchen cooking up a meal for us. Such hands-on entrepreneurship is typical in outlying areas of the world.

There was some striking differences between the Mekong here and the Irrawaddy further west in Myanmar. The Mekong mid-section has more limestone hills, looking rather pristine with lots of green jungle, though Bill was quick to point out that these were not primary forest but secondary growth. We rarely saw any birds or heard much cricket and insect chirping at night. Fish life along the Mekong was also relatively scanty, though we managed to buy a five kilo goonch catfish, measuring almost a meter in length.

岸邊看到一棵被砍倒的大樹。

沿著湄公河往下游去，花了兩天時間我們才抵達龍坡邦。
這裡曾經是寮國的首都，現在卻有個奇怪的新政策，要求
所有觀光船必須停靠在離世界遺址北邊十公里的地方，然
後，再由嘟嘟車、三輪摩托車載著旅客進城；沒有載客的
空船可以一路行駛到城裡停靠。唯一可以想到的理由，不
管合不合乎邏輯，我推斷一定是某高官運作的組織，刻意
製造旅客的不便，然後從中賺取一筆費用。

這時是旅遊的淡季，很多旅社民宿都沒開門。我們找到一
間靠河岸的小型旅社，七間空房，剛好可以給我們十二個
人住。我們包下整個 *Muong Lao Riverside* 飯店，一間房一
晚只要十七點五美元。從我 203 號房的陽台看出去，湄
公河就在眼前。我看到一位年輕人就在對街幫人剪頭髮。
下樓去瞧瞧，我的頭髮也需要剪了。結果這理髮師是我
們飯店的經理，只是幫朋友的忙。很快的，我也坐在凳子
上，成為他的朋友，剪了個免費的頭。

飯店櫃檯貼著一張標示「*Wifi* 密碼 *Daniel117*」。我跟櫃
台的年輕女孩聊起天，「*Daniel* 是飯店的老闆嗎？」我問。
「*Daniel* 是我的名字。」年輕女孩微笑的回我，酒窩都跑
出來了。「*Daniel*？但是那是男生的名字耶」我大呼。「在
寮國語裡，我的名字聽起來就像 *Daniel*，所以我選這個名

On two occasions however, I saw an elephant.

Villagers here tend not to bathe in the river or wash their clothes along the banks, unlike people living along the Irrawaddy. There was little river traffic save local ferries and small fishing sampans. The river was not wide, and the banks offered little farmland. Plantings were mainly up the hillside, using slash and burn rotation for crops like corn, beans and sticky dry rice. While I saw no dams, I did see a huge tree being cut down by the bank.

After two long days sailing downriver on the Mekong, we reached Luang Prabang. A strange new policy had been implemented recently forcing all tourist boats to dock ten kilometers north of the World Heritage city, once the capital of Laos. Tuk-tuks, designated motor tricycles, would then take the tourists into town, while the boats were allowed to sail empty of passengers all the way to the town center where they moored along the banks. The only reason, logical or illogical, I could deduce was that some officials were running

字！」Daniel 用著不流暢的英文解釋。她十九歲，飯店是她父母的。她的姊姊在成都的大學讀旅遊系，三年級生。

往上游去，我用 iPad 查看衛星照片。基於 Deang 對這區域的熟悉，我決定我們應該往南塔河走，那是湄公河重要的支流之一，然後到瑯南塔，我們停車的地方。坐小的長尾木船估計要兩天的時間。因為我們需要兩艘船容納十二個人，Deang 事先打了電話安排。離開龍坡邦的第二天，我們到了巴塔的合流點，兩艘船已經在岸邊等候我們了。此刻，我們帶上船的零食已經全部被消滅了。

第一天坐了十小時的小船，歷經暴風雨，我們抵達 Khon Kham 村。來自紐西蘭的捐款，幫這村子蓋了一個環保屋。我們十二個人全都不算是身材標準的，排排躺好在這兩個房間的地上。這裡幾乎沒什麼食物也沒有餐廳，所以我們帶著先前買的一隻鴨跟雞，宰殺後開始準備晚餐。當地的寮國婦女的編織技術真是好，她們的商品很快的被團員買走，剛好大家也想要把剩下的寮國錢花掉，因為旅途即將結束。我自己也買了好幾件，舊的新的都買。最吸引我的是一塊織得很漂亮的布，上面有許多動物跟鳥的圖騰。

最後，七天的旅程，行走在湄公河跟支流南塔河上，即將接近終點瑯南塔省。河流窄，水很急。在幾個地方，水流像急流泛舟那樣，得小心的逆著水流前進，時不時河水會

some kind of syndicate to inconvenience tourists while extracting a higher than usual fare to enter the heritage site.

It was low season for tourism and many hostels and Bed & Breakfast lodges were closed for business. We found one small family hotel by the bank of the river. With seven vacant rooms, it was just the perfect size for our team of twelve. We took up the entire Muong Lao Riverside Hotel, costing only USD17.5 per room. From my balcony in Room 203, I could view the Mekong flowing by. Just across the street, I noticed a young man was cutting the hair of another man. I went down the stairs and checked it out, as I too badly needed a cut. It turned out the barber was the manager of our hotel, doing a favor for a friend. Soon I took up the stool, became his friend, and got my free haircut.

Posted on our hotel reception was a sign, "Wifi password – Daniel1177." I chatted with the young lady at the reception desk. "Is Daniel the owner of this hotel?" I asked. "Daniel is my name," answered the lady with a smile showing her dimples. "Daniel? But that's a guy's name!" I exclaimed. "In Lao language, my name sounded exactly like Daniel, so I chose that name," Daniel explained with halting English. She is 19 years old and the hotel belongs to her parents. Her elder sister is a third year student studying tourism at a university in Chengdu.

Muong Lao Hotel / 下榻的 Muong Lao 旅社

On our way back upriver, I checked on satellite images with my iPad. I decided, together with Deang's knowledge of the area, that we should be able to sail up the Namtha River, an important tributary of the Mekong, to Luang Namtha where our cars were parked. It should take two days on small long-tail wooden boats. As we needed two boats to accommodate all twelve of us, Deang called ahead, and two boats were ready when we reached the confluence at Pak Tha on the second day after leaving Luang Prabang. By now the junk food we brought along on our boat was about depleted.

The first day after ten hours on the small boat through torrential rain ended at Khon Kham Village. Volunteers from New Zealand had donated funds and helped build an eco-lodge. All twelve of us barely fit, lined up on the floor in two rooms. Hardly any food was available and there were no restaurants, so we bought and had one duck and one chicken slaughtered to prepare for our dinner. The local Lao women were excellent weavers. Their wares were soon snatched up by our eager group trying to expend the remaining Kip that we had exchanged, as we were nearing the end of our trip. I too, bought several pieces, both old and new ones. I was particularly attracted to one exquisite woven fabric with many animal and bird motifs.

Finally, after seven days on the Mekong and its tributary the Namtha, we were on the last leg towards reaching Luang Namtha. The river had narrowed to a fast running stream. At several locations, it dropped in

濺到我們的小船上。有些時候我沒有辦法分辨濺到我們身上的是河水還是雨水。

好不容易我上岸了，兩隻腳站在南塔河的岸上。回到飯店，我發現自己還在晃，好像我還在河上。晚餐後，我決定喝兩杯酒，雖然我的酒量只有一杯。我想如果我還是繼續暈，最好是因為酒精而不是因為這七天待在船上。這個幻想對一個五歲的小孩可能管用，但對一位已經六十五歲的人，是時候回到現實了。

rapids like those for whitewater rafting, and we proceeded with trepidation against the current. These were also occasions when the water would splash into our tiny boat. At times, I could not determine which was making us soaking wet, the river or the rain.

At long last, I was back on land, with my two feet anchored on the bank of the Namtha River. Back at our hotel, I found myself swaying from side to side, as if I were still on the river. At dinner, I decided to have two glasses of wine, though my usual tolerance would be one. I figured that, if I must feel dizzy, I might feel better thinking that it was from the wine rather than from being on boats for seven days. While that might work well with the imagination of a five year old child, I found that it was time for a reality check, for someone at 65.

密西西比河源頭

TO THE SOURCE OF THE MISSISSIPPI

Lake Itasca, Minnesota – September 18, 2015

密西西比河源頭

北緯 47.24° ／西經 95.20° ／ 海拔 1475 呎／
2015 年 9 月 18 日 9:44 分

夢想了好多年、花了好幾個月的時間做規劃、好幾週的時間做準備、加上出發前幾天的興奮……在尋找亞洲重要河流源頭的探險裡，出發前的過程都是這樣的，並且這些河流的源頭幾乎全部都在西藏高原上。找到地理上真正的源頭前，在可以定位在地圖上，雙腳真正站上那個源頭前，必須經過許多煎熬：開車，騎馬，徒步前往想像中的源頭。緊接著是那歷史的一刻，喝下一口源頭的水，滿足了心理與腦袋的渴。對我個人來說，這個過程被複製了幾遍；長江〈1985，1995，2005〉、湄公河〈2007〉、黃河〈2008〉，還有薩爾溫江〈2011〉。

不過我去密西西比河的源頭卻是臨時起意的，也許跟兩天前坐在威斯康辛州和明尼蘇達州間的密西西比河上有關；這條河是世界上第四長的河。從明尼蘇達州雙城聖保羅，也就是我待的地方，到艾塔斯卡湖（雄偉的密西西比河的上游跟源頭），整個旅途只需要開一百八十英里，而且沿途的路鋪的很好。從源頭開始直到墨西哥灣出海，全長 2,320 英里。

TO THE SOURCE OF THE MISSISSIPPI

47.24°N 95.20°W Elevation 1475 Feet 9:44 September 18, 2015

It takes years of dreaming, months of planning, weeks of preparation, and days of final excitement, before launching an expedition to the source of any great river of Asia; almost all of them are on the Tibetan plateau. Not to speak of the grueling days of driving, riding and hiking toward an imagined river source before that final step makes it a real geographic spot for both the map and your feet. Then there is that historic moment of satisfaction quenching both the mind and the heart with a drink from the source. For me, that process has been repeated several times; for the Yangtze (1985, 1995, 2005), the Mekong (2007), the Yellow River (2008) and the Salween (2011).

But my journey to the source of the Mississippi, fourth longest river in the world, began on the spur of the moment, perhaps in a dream two days ago while sailing on a motorboat on the Mississippi between Wisconsin and Minnesota. It may seem anticlimactic, as the journey was a meager 180 mile drive on good roads, from the Twin Cities of Minneapolis/St Paul where I was staying to Lake Itasca, known as headwaters and source of the mighty Mississippi. There, the river begins its 2,320 mile journey to the ocean in the

從歷史上來看，密西西比河的源頭並不像細水那樣平靜，它在十九世紀時很神秘，也很受爭議。美國的原住民，對當地的地理非常熟悉，尤其是住在明尼蘇達州北部的齊佩瓦族。他們世世代代的祖先早在這裡遨遊。透過他們的指引，早期到美國定居的人，由探險家或地理學家帶領，經過一連串的遠征才找到密西西比河的源頭。追求能成為第一個找到源頭的人，這計謀就好像是本小說。

對我這個探險家來說，我覺得密西西比河源頭最有趣的地方並不是它的發現，而是在歷史上有不同團體爭相去為源頭定位而引起的爭論。也或許正是這樣，幾世紀以來，地理學家，探險家，冒險家，都得要面對這地理上的挑戰。

亨利‧斯庫爾克拉夫特（*Henry Schoolcraft*），是位地

Gulf of Mexico.

Historically the journey to the Mississippi source was not as calm as a trickle, and instead was wrapped in mystery and controversy during the 19th Century. Native Americans, in particular the Chippewa living in northern Minnesota, knew the local geography well. For generations their ancestors roamed this land. It was through their guidance that early settlers in America, led by the explorer/geographers of their day, finally pinpointed the source of the Mississippi through a sequence of challenging expeditions. The intrigue involved in pursuit of the honor of being the first to discover the source unveiled itself like fiction.

For me as an explorer, what I found most fascinating about the source of the Mississippi is not so much the discovery, but the historical controversy and contention among different parties in their attempts to define the source. This is perhaps true for many major geographical challenges facing geographers, explorers and adventurers throughout the centuries to this day.

Henry Schoolcraft, a geographer, geologist and ethnologist was generally accepted as the person who first led an expedition in 1832 to Lake Itasca and defined that body of water as the headwaters and source of the Mississippi. But the controversy that developed around the claim of a "gentleman" by the name of Willard Glazier is most intriguing. In 1881, Glazier's party wanted

Tug with barges on river / 河上的拖船

理學家，也是地質學家和民族學家，他普遍被認為是第一個去探源的人，1832 年他到了艾塔斯卡湖，將這湖水定義為源頭，密西西比河的源頭。然而有趣的事發生了，爭議由一位名為 Willard Glazier 的「紳士」而起。1881 年，Glazier 一群人想要成為第一支探險隊伍，他們從密西西比河的源頭航行到出海口，整個行程花了他一百一十七天。他在到了艾塔斯卡湖後，又往前行進了一些，發現了另外一個比較高的湖，這個湖水往下注入艾塔斯卡湖。他於是將這湖命名為 Glazier Lake，他自己的名字，宣稱這才是真正的源頭。

不過當時學術團體的「紳士們」並不接受這樣的說法。名不經傳的冒險家居然講得出這樣的話，這是多麼的荒謬啊！將軍詹姆士‧貝克被明尼蘇達歷史學會指派去調查這個說法。貝克將軍不僅表示 Glazier 湖其實就是大家早已知道的麋鹿湖（Elk Lake），他也揭穿這個自我吹捧，又厚臉皮的傢伙是個幌子。事實上，有很多的小湖已經被命名了，也知道湖水會流向艾塔斯卡湖，這湖就像是蓄水池，也是密西西比河的源頭。

在貝克將軍給學會的報告裡，他用了這些字眼去形容 Glazier：「愚蠢的」、「自命不凡的」、「可恥的」、「詐騙」、「騙子」、「剽竊者」、「觀光遊客」、「文學的小偷」、「偽造歷史」、「假的探險家」、「虛假的

to become the first to sail down the entire Mississippi river from its source to its mouth, an attempt that finally took him 117 days. While tackling the headwaters, he went to Lake Itasca and a little beyond, identifying a slightly higher lake which drains into Lake Itasca. He named it Glazier Lake, and not only claimed it as his own, but claimed that it was the real source.

But other "gentlemen" among learned societies of the time would not have it that way. How preposterous that a never-heard-of adventurer could come up with such a claim! A General James Baker was assigned by the Minnesota Historical Society to investigate the new claims. Not only did Baker testify that Glazier's lake had long been known as Elk Lake, he lobbed accusations that Glazier, an unabashed self-promoter, was a fake. After all, many smaller lakes, with various names already assigned, were known to feed into Itasca Lake, which serves as a reservoir of water considered as the headwaters of the Mississippi.

In his report to the Society, he called Glazier "stupid", "pretentious", "shameful", "a fraud", "a liar", "a Plagiarist", "a tourist", "a literary thief", "a falsifier of history", "a quack explorer", "a charlatan adventurer", "a merry fellow on a jolly outing", and more. He felt that Glazier had not worked hard enough to find the source and thus did not deserve the merit. Only a learned man should have claimed such an important discovery!

Old steamboat on lake / 湖邊的老蒸汽船

Adding salt to the wound, the report further described how Glazier, "travels 155 miles by railroad car to the city of Brainerd in one night, and doubtless in a sleeping car. And all this through a region over which Nicollet [an explorer who came almost half a century earlier] had toiled weeks and months with all the privation incidents to an untrodden wilderness." He went on to say that Glazier traveled over "established road and portages", and this could hardly be considered true exploration. He further humiliated Glazier as a lousy shot, who shot at everything and barely got any real game meat.

The Minnesota Historical Society went as far as requesting all organizations that printed their maps with Glazier Lake to erase that name, and instead put Elk Lake in its place. Thus a somewhat intrepid person with perhaps too eager a wish for fame was written off, though his claim at the time, as well as for now, was largely correct.

冒險家」、「快樂傢伙的歡樂旅行」，還有更多。他覺得
Glazier 並沒有用功也不值得被稱讚。只有學者才有資格
去發表這樣的發現！

在傷口上再撒些鹽吧，報告裡進一步說明 Glazier「不用
懷疑，他一定搭了夜班火車，移動了 155 英里到達布雷
納德（Brainerd）。這個旅程花了約瑟夫·尼柯萊特（一位
差不多是半世紀之前的探險家）好幾個月的時間，經歷許
多困苦才來到這個尚未被發掘的地方。」他又說 Glazier
「行走在鋪好的路，還找搬運工」，這樣算哪門子的探險。
他繼續羞辱 Glazier，說他的槍法很糟，開一堆槍也獵不
到什麼東西。

明尼蘇達歷史學會採取更多的動作，要求所有的團體把他
們地圖上的 Glazier Lake 改成 Elk Lake。這樣做也許會讓
這個太想要出名的傢伙從歷史上除名，但是 Glazier 在當
時所說的話，到現在大部分還是成立的。

如果那時候 Glazier 旅行的方式不配當一個探險家，而
我現今旅行的方式：舒適又亮眼的四輪驅動凱迪拉克
Escalade Platinum、可以加溫跟調整角度的座椅、超過
180 英里的路都是鋪好的，還有嚮導是 GPS 而不是印地
安人；對一個探險家來說，這應該被視為最墮落，最不恥
也是最不適當的方式。但，那樣旅行的方式只會把我侷限

If Glazier's method of travel was put into question in his days as not worthy of an explorer, my own contemporary travel, in a posh Cadillac all-wheel-drive Escalade Platinum edition with heated and reclining seats, over 180 miles of paved road, with GPS rather than Indian guidance, must be considered the utmost of decadence, disgraceful and unbecoming of an explorer by any definition. That style of travel would put me squarely in the category of an ex-explorer.

But that was exactly what I did! With my college friend Victor Chan behind the wheels, his wife Lonio on logistics in charge of junk food snacks, Xavier our filmmaker to record my fifth journey to a river source, and Berry as designated backseat jet-lag napper, we stopped first at the "tourist center" to pay the $5 entrance fee to Itasca State Park, first state park of Minnesota.

Checking into a three-room cabin lodge with flushing toilet and a shower could hardly be qualified as basecamp. Outside temperature lingered at 60°F whereas inside the heater was turned up to 72°F. The fireplace, filled with a cord of firewood, was left unlit, though it would have added amber to warmth. An enclosed porch with rocking chairs looked down upon Itasca Lake just a hundred yards or so away. What a contrast to the tent camps in sub-zero temperatures and snowstorms my team and I were so used to braving in our journey to the other river sources of Asia! A good night's sleep prepared us for the "charge" to the Mississippi source the next morning!

為一個過氣的探險家。

對！我確是這樣去旅行的。我的老同學陳大緣駕車，他老婆 Lonio 負責零食的補給，Xavier 負責製作我們的影片，這趟是來製作我第五次追溯河流源頭的過程；我後座乘客 Berry 則負責調整時差睡大覺，我們在旅客中心暫停，付了 $5 的門票進入艾塔斯卡湖，明尼蘇達州的第一個州立公園。

住進配有沖水馬桶跟衛浴設備的三房小木屋民宿，根本稱不上在戶外的大本營。外面的溫度徘徊在華氏 60°，而室內的暖氣溫度調到 72°。壁爐內放滿了柴火，還沒點著，點著後會讓屋子裡面感覺更溫暖。室內陽台上有個搖椅，對著約一百碼的地方往下看就是艾塔斯卡湖。我跟團隊在探亞洲幾條河流源頭時，紮營的地方氣溫都在攝氏零下，也歷經暴風雪，與此刻相比，是多大的反差。一夜的好眠，讓我們隔天早上可以好好地往密西西比河的源頭前進。

就當艾塔斯卡湖上的霧漸漸消失，我們去 Douglas Lodge 的餐廳吃了豐盛的早餐。之後我們開了八英里到達湖的北邊，木頭做成的指示牌上明顯的標出湖的出口，並指向一條河川涇流，也就是源頭的方向。我穿上最喜歡的奧地利外套，好像才剛開完一個正式的會議一樣，我慎重的脫掉鞋子，把腳泡進冰凍的水裡感覺好奇妙。我從來不敢在亞

Just as the morning mist was lifting from Lake Itasca, we went for a hearty breakfast at the Douglas Lodge restaurant. Afterwards, we drove for eight miles to the northern end of Itasca Lake where a well-marked piece of timber designates the exit of the lake into a run-off stream as the source of the Mississippi River. Sporting my favorite Austrian jacket, as if coming out of a business meeting, I solemnly took off my shoes. Dipping my feet into the somewhat chilly water was still magical. After all, this is a feat I would not dare to attempt at other river sources of Asia; they all originate from glacial water of the high plateau.

With small steps, I gingerly crossed the twenty feet or so of the stream to the other bank, testing the smoothed rocks beneath my feet. I had done something figuratively monumental, crossing the mighty Mississippi River on foot! Alas, there was no Moet Chandon this time around to toast our arrival at a great river source. Even a bottle of cheaper champagne might seem an overkill, given the ease I had taken to arrive here. We lingered only long enough to have a few pictures taken before driving onward on a 17-mile loop around the lake.

At one point, we passed by Nicollet Creek, a tiny stream which drains into Lake Itasca, considered by some as the real source. Joseph Nicollet was deemed one of the explorers of the early 1800s who had contributed to geographic knowledge of the Mississippi source, leading an expedition to the

洲河流的源頭幹這種事，因為他們都源自高原上的冰河。

我小心翼翼地橫跨約二十呎的寬度到河的對岸，一小步一小步的測試我腳下光滑的岩石。我剛做了一件了不起的事，用雙腳橫跨密西西比河！啊，這次沒有 *Moet Chandon* 的香檳來慶祝我們抵達這偉大河流的源頭。但即使是一瓶普通廉價的香檳也顯得過份，畢竟我是這麼輕鬆的就來到這裡。我們只在這裡待了一會兒，拍了些照片，然後就往下繞著湖開了十七英哩。

一度我們經過 *Nicollet Creek*，那是條流向艾塔斯卡湖的小溪，有些人認為這才是真正的源頭。瑟夫·尼柯萊特（*Joseph Nicollet*）是 *1800s* 年初期的探險家，*1836* 年就去了這個區域探險，他貢獻了密西西比河源頭地區地理上的知識。再往前一點，我們到了麋鹿湖（*Elk Lake*）。麋鹿湖距離艾塔斯卡湖只有幾百碼，有條小溪連接了一個高一點的湖跟另一個低一點的湖。這也是為什麼 *Glazier* 主張麋鹿湖才是源頭，而不是艾塔斯卡湖。

不一會兒我們回到 *Douglas Lodge*。我在櫃檯寫了張名信片，也寄了。在網路時代，我想不到要將名信片寄給誰。最後我決定寄給我自己，當作這天在源頭的紀念。

也許再過一世紀，西藏高原上的河川源頭命運也會跟密

region in 1836. Just a little further and we were at Elk Lake. At this point, Elk Lake was only a few hundred yards from Itasca Lake, with a small stream leading from the slightly higher former lake to the latter. Thus was the basis for the assertion by Glazier that Elk Lake trumps Itasca.

Before too long, we were back at Douglas Lodge. I stopped by the reception area to write a post card and mail it. With our internet age, I could not think of anyone to mail this postcard to. Finally I decided best to post it to myself, as a memory of this very special day at the Mississippi source.

Perhaps in another century, other river sources of Asia may face the same fate as that of the Mississippi source - with a paved road driving up to a glamorous five-star hotel, checking into a room with hot shower fed by heated glacial water from the Tibetan mountains. This would be a worthy tribute to Willard

西西比河源頭一樣，路鋪得好好的，直達五星級飯店，
再把冰河的水加熱，好讓每間房都有熱水可以用。這算
是我對 *Willard Glazier* 的致敬，雖然他在源頭的定義上
有爭議，而現在的我離那裏如此靠近，北緯 *47.24°*／西
經 *95.20°*／海拔 *1475* 呎。

Glazier who first, though disputably, defined the source of the Mississippi, a short distance from where I stood today at 47.24°N and 95.20°W, and 1475 feet in elevation.

Nicollet creek / Nicollet 溪

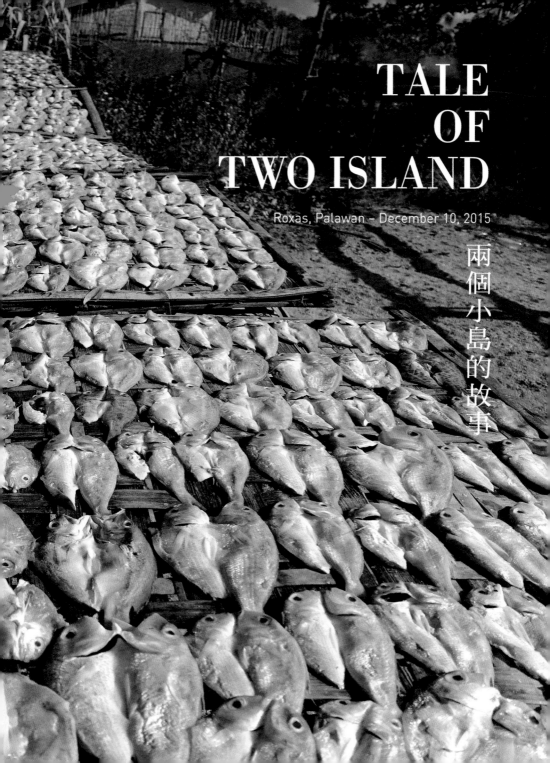

TALE
OF
TWO ISLAND

Roxas, Palawan – December 10, 2015

兩個小島的故事

兩個小島的故事 順便尋找尼莫

離開香港緊湊腳步的生活，我與團隊回到菲律賓南部的巴拉望，這裡的時間很慢，日子很長，只有在這種環境我才可以在晚上聽到森林裡演奏的歌曲與交響樂。我把助手 *Jocelyn* 的家當作我們的臨時基地：兩間竹子房。屋外小孩們正在玩我小時候同樣的遊戲，在泥土地上彈珠子。玩這遊戲所需的技巧已隨著年紀的增長而逐漸遠離我了，但卻引發了許多回憶。很快的，我們出海了。

「再過兩個月農曆新年到時，這些魚會變得很值錢。」*Goeray* 指著漁網裡滿滿的紅石斑說。*Goeray* 是 *Johnson Island* 這裡「魚與珊瑚保護區」的保全人員。「賣給貿易商銷往香港，一公斤要價大概 *3000* 比索！」*Goeray* 又說。那差不多是港幣五百塊錢，這只是當地的行情，若是賣到街上又會乘上幾倍，餐廳裡當然就更貴了。

漁網裡大約有二十尾的魚，很漂亮，有些粉紅，有些紅，有些深紅，全部都有好可愛的斑點。大尾的約一英尺長，小一點的也有四分之三大。再過幾個月牠們會長到 *1.5* 公

A TALE OF TWO ISLANDS
and finding Nemo

Finally after all the rush rush of Hong Kong, my team of ten and I are back in Palawan in the southern Philippines, where time is slow and days are long. Only under such circumstances I would again hear the songs and symphony of the forest in the night. At my helper Jocelyn's home, now made into our temporary operation base with two purpose-built bamboo houses, I observed kids playing my own childhood game of marble in the dirt courtyard. My knack for it has long been lost to age, but it brought back fond memories. Soon we were all out at sea.

"When Chinese New Year comes, in about two months, these fish will be worth a lot," said Goeray, who is security officer of the fish and coral sanctuary of Johnson Island. He was referring to a net full of Red Garoupa. "When sold to merchant collectors destined for Hong Kong, one kilo would be worth around 3000 peso," Goeray added. That would translate into roughly HKD500. And that is the local price here. The street price would be a multiple of that, and restaurant prices still higher.

Red Garoupa in net / 網中的紅石斑

Inside the net were about twenty beautiful fish, some pink and others red or redder, all with some lovely spots. Large ones were about one foot long and smaller ones at three-quarter that size. In another couple months, they would be weighing in around 1.5 kilos each, ready for the market. But for now they must be fed once every three days. For luck or fortune, Chinese would want a Red Garoupa, cooked from a live fish and served on the table, thus driving the prices to its highest during that festive season.

Today, Goeray and his fellow villagers are transferring the fish from a large net to a huge cage, measuring roughly six-foot square, as high as a person. This netted cage was pushed off from the stern of their boat and sank quickly to the bottom, maybe six meters below the surface. One fellow transferred all the garoupa into a smaller net held in one hand, and in his other hand was a plastic bag of a chopped up stingray he caught earlier in the morning. The ray fish would become today's meal for the garoupa.

Another small boat momentarily moored beside us and I could hear a generator kick in, driving a compressor connected to a small plastic tube thrown into the water. The same fellow, now with simple face goggle and homemade flippers, grabbed the tube and put it in his mouth. Quickly, he dived and went under. I could see the bubbles coming to the top and realized he had gone slightly to the left of our boat.

斤，可以上市了。不過現在牠們必須每三天被餵食一次。估計是為了好運，中國人喜歡用活的紅石斑來烹煮，這讓價錢在節慶時又更貴了。

此刻 *Goeray* 跟幾位村民正將魚從大漁網移到六英尺平方的大籠子，大約有一個人那麼高。網狀的籠子從船上卸下，馬上就沉到了大概有六米深的海底。其中一人將所有的紅石斑移到他手上的小漁網，另一手則拿著一袋他早上捕獲的魟魚，已經被大卸八塊的魟魚，今天成為紅石斑的餐點。

一艘小船暫時停靠在我們旁邊，我聽見發電機開始運作，壓縮機接著一根小塑膠管，管子被丟進水裡。剛剛在餵紅石斑的那個人現在正戴著簡易的護目鏡跟自己做的蛙鞋進到水裡，然後他把塑膠管抓過來放進嘴裡。很快地，他潛下水。看到浮上水面的氣泡，我知道他正在我們船的左邊。

他潛進那個大水箱裡，那些紅石斑將會被轉移來到這裡。魚還在長大，需要足夠的空間活動才會健康，然後，再過兩個月牠們就會被空運到香港販賣了。那個人潛下去有三、四分鐘，還有個沒配戴潛水器具的男子在水裡幫他。大約又過一分鐘，兩個人才浮上水面，大功告成。

Red Garoupa ready for market / 準備運送到市場的紅石斑

He was going down with the garoupa to be released inside the larger tank. They are growing in size and needed more room to remain healthy, in time to be flown to Hong Kong for sale in less than two months. He must be down there for three to four minutes while another young man free-dived down to assist him. In another minute or so, both men surfaced, and the job was done.

Perhaps the job has been done too well, as everyone admitted that the red garoupa are getting harder and harder to come by. Put simply, coral fish are being fished out, due to an insatiable demand for seafood by the growing Chinese market. Sooner or later, their Dream of the Red Chamber would burst.

We are here just a couple hundred meters off Johnson Island, a pristine island

也許大家都把這份工作做得太好了，因此每個人也都承認紅石斑是越來越難捕獲了；換句話說，因為中國市場的需求不斷擴大，因此珊瑚魚已經被過度捕撈了。不久，這些人的「紅」樓夢將會毀滅。

我們離 Johnson Island 只有幾百公尺，潔淨的小島，水很透徹，珊瑚礁很漂亮，村民保護的很好。島上有一百五十戶人家，約五百多個居民。若是在這裡詢問他們的人口數，他們的回答是所有大人的總數，也就是二十一歲以上可以投票的人，不知道為什麼小孩跟青少年沒被算進去。

儘管房子簡陋，這個村子很有秩序也很乾淨，街道也都有人打掃。有幾口大家共用的水井，一間破舊但很乾淨的教堂。人們很善良也很熱心助人。我們禮拜六下午到了後，買了些魚、螃蟹，還有琵琶蝦。兩公斤的螃蟹花我們三百比索，十一隻琵琶蝦四百比索，非常划算，買家賣家都開心。

接近傍晚的時候，女士們在庭院裡的臨時球場玩起排球。男子則是分成好幾組在學校旁的水泥地上打籃球。我們也組了一隊跟當地人比賽，結果我們輸了一分跟一百五十比索。小孩們若不是在看我們比賽，就是踩著自己用木頭做的高蹺在附近走來走去。

with clear ocean water and beautiful coral reefs, protected by the villagers. On the island are some 150 families and 500 plus residents. Here, when asked about population numbers, it is generally answered by tallying up the adults, or those eligible to vote above 21 years of age. Children and teenagers are somehow not part of the statistics.

The village was very orderly and clean, despite houses being simple and basic. The streets are obviously swept all the time. Freshwater was provided by several communal wells. The single church, though Spartan, was spotlessly clean. The people were very friendly and helpful. We arrived on a Saturday afternoon and were able to purchase some fish, crab, and even slipper lobster. Two kilos of crab cost us 300 peso and eleven slipper lobster 400 peso, a huge

Ray at sunrise / 海上的曙光

bargain. Both buyer and seller were very happy.

Toward evening, the ladies were playing a game of volley ball in a make-shift court. The men, on the other hand, were divided into several teams and played basketball in the only cement court by the school. Our crew formed a team and challenged the villagers. We lost by one point and left 150 peso poorer. Children were either watching the games, or walking around on wooden stilts they made from simple wood and nails.

Tomorrow would be Sunday. After church, the weekly cock fight would preoccupy the men of the village. Almost every home has caged areas where spectacularly groomed cocks reside, their heads rising high, ready for the next engagement.

Though winter monsoon had arrived and at times we had to brave some two-meter swell, we embarked in two boats, staying onboard for one week. Every morning sunrise and evening sunset were a most rewarding experience at sea. We sailed to Johnson Island and a group of small islets off the coast of Roxas, a town along the east coast of Palawan. I have divided groups of small islands along the east coast as focus for our future voyage of discovery, being careful to avoid the hot water and the Spratly toward the west coast.

Some of the most beautiful islands here are made into resorts, privately

明天就是禮拜天了，上完教堂後，村裡的男人全跑去鬥雞。這裡幾乎每一家都有放雞籠的地方，鬥雞公也都被照顧的很好。神氣的把頭抬高，準備迎接下一場的挑戰。

雖然冬天的雨季已經到來，但是有時候浪還是會打到兩米高，我們登上兩艘船，要在船上待上一個星期。每個早晨的日出和每個傍晚的日落在海上顯得格外美麗。我們開到 *Johnson Island* 跟一些沿著 *Roxas* 海岸的小島，還有一個在巴拉望東海岸的小鎮。我將東岸的小島分成幾組，這些未來都是我們會探索的目標，我也很小心的避開近來爭議不斷，靠西岸的南沙群島。

有些非常漂亮的小島都變成了私人的度假村，只有住在那裡的人才可以進入。小島的價錢並非那麼令人望而卻步，大約美金一百萬。對我們這些習慣香港天價地產的人來說，買個私人的小島顯得挺划算的。

停泊在 *Johnson Island* 只需要一百五十比索，也就是港幣二十五元。我們的船 *HM Explorer 2*，上面有六位船員照顧我們；另一艘船稍微小一點，有三位船員照顧三位客人。雖然三位年長的船員都六十多歲了，但他們射魚的功夫可真是了得。不需要任何潛水工具，一下子就潛到五米或更深的地方，浮上水面時也把我們的午餐或晚餐帶上來。他們的體力跟精力真是令人佩服，尤其我的年

owned. Visitors are not allowed on them unless they sign up to stay there. Prices for such small islands are however not prohibitive, roughly a million USD or thereabout. For those of us used to astronomical prices of Hong Kong's housing, it seemed rather affordable to own an entire island.

We were charged the meager sum of 150 peso as anchoring fee at Johnson Island. That is a pittance of HKD25. On our boat HM Explorer 2, we have six in the crew serving seven of us. The other boat, slightly smaller, has three crew serving three guests. Three of the more senior boatmen, all well into the sixties, were excellent in spearing fish. Free diving to a depth of five meters and more, they would bring back fish for lunch or dinner. Their stamina and energy were a humbling experience for me, being their contemporary in age.

One particular catch was of high significance, a half kilo Leopard Garoupa, locally called more beautifully as Señorita. This all-white color fish has black spots over its body. In Hong Kong, they are known as the Rat Garoupa, an ugly name yet commanding a hefty sum. These days, maybe over a decade already, one simply hears about such fish, but never seen them in restaurant tanks or served at table. They have, again, been fished out.

While the one we got was very much alive throughout the day, hung from a line off the side of our boat, it died the next morning and the body turned gray. I was shocked that beautiful señorita has turned into ugly señora. And

紀和他們相仿。

有一條他們抓到的魚別具意義，那是半公斤重的豹斑，當地人叫的名字比較好聽：「小姐」。小姐全身白色帶著黑色斑點，香港人叫老鼠斑，名字不好聽但是卻貴的不得了。近來，也許近十年來，大家只有聽過卻不曾在餐桌上見過牠，當然也是被過度的捕獵的犧牲品。

我們捕到的這傢伙一整天都很有活力，便把牠放在船邊，但是隔天牠死了而且變成灰色。我很訝異這麼漂亮的小姐竟變成醜陋的小姐。而更讓我驚訝的是，船員居然把牠拿去炭烤而不是清蒸！

下一個村莊 Shell Island，離 Johnson Island 只有六公里，兩地的人口組成相似。但是這兩個社區截然不同。當橡皮艇一上岸，我們就去社區區長那裡申請靠岸跟過夜的許可。

村子很頹廢很亂，到處是垃圾，破舊的船、漁網被隨意丟在海岸上，屋子旁。許多房子失修，茅草屋頂上都是補丁，竹牆也剝落。總之跟我們剛去的 Johnson Island 真是天壤地別。

問過之後才知道部分的原因，原來這個漁村被禁止捕魚兩

more shocked that the crew grilled it with charcoal rather than steam it!

While island hopping, the next village we visited was Shell Island, barely six kilometers away and with a similar population make-up as Johnson. But the two communities could not be more different. Once ashore with our Zodiac inflatables, we went first to get permission from the president of the community, to anchor and spend the night here.

The village looked dilapidated and arranged in disorder. Much refuse were left around, old broken boats and nets were abandoned around the shore and next to houses. Many of these houses were in disrepair, with patchy thatched roofs and worn bamboo sidings. In all, it was a huge contrast from Johnson Island where we had just been.

Upon inquiry, we found out part of the reason was that the community, a fishing village, was not allowed to fish for two years already. There had been a ban by government, in particular the Marine Police, prohibiting the villagers from further fishing. It stemmed from them being repeatedly caught dredging the bay with long fishing nets that destroyed much of the nearby coral. All the fishing boats being tied down along the shore were actually "grounded".

Shell Island used to be famous also for its abalone. But quick and unsustainable harvest based on greed turned this asset into a dead end as

年了。政府的命令，尤其是從海警下的，禁止村民進行任何捕撈。這是因為他們一直都會用長長的漁網拖魚，這動作破壞了許多珊瑚礁。因此這裡所有的船都被綁在岸邊，真的被禁足了。

Shell Island 原本因為出產鮑魚而出名。這種貪心，只顧眼前利益的過度的捕撈讓這裡的資源消失，漁夫們為了捕鮑魚總是把珊瑚翻的亂七八糟。今天，連最常出沒在珊瑚礁的珊瑚魚都不見了。

近來他們會趁海警下班的時候，偷偷地在夜晚出海捕魚。在 Roxas 有個魚的買家，每回看到海警的巡邏船開出港口，就會馬上跟他們通風報信。

這種貓抓老鼠的遊戲讓這裡更沒有東西可以捕，偶爾被抓到的話，漁網會被充公。這兩年來狀況越來越差，村子變得越來越窮也越來越破舊，但好像也沒有解決的方案。現在這些村民靠著捕捉沿岸的小漁獲維生，將牠們曬乾，為單調的飲食添些小菜。

這些小島給了我們很多次潛水的機會。雖然沒有整套的配備，但我們浮潛得很快活，並且難得的看到了這裡美麗的熱帶魚。我們從昆明來的探洞團隊，他們原本是對陸地底下的世界熟悉，但來到這裡變成了水底下的專家。畢博士

fishermen turned the coral upside down to look for the abalone. Today, even the coral fish that used to frequent the island are largely gone.

These days, they would sneak out and fish in the darkness of night, especially on the weekend when the Marine Police would be off duty. A fish collector from Roxas would also call them to give advance notice if he saw the marine patrol were to leave harbor.

Such cat and mouse game left the villagers with much less catch, as well as occasionally being caught and having their nets confiscated. Conditions had deteriorated over a two year period, thus the village had become more and more poor and rundown. There seemed no solution in sight as villagers subsisted on small catch near shore, drying these fish to supplement their already monotonous diet.

In between visiting islands, we made many dives. Though without full equipment, simply snorkeling around the many near-surface coral heads offered exceptional viewing opportunity of all the beautiful tropical fish of the area. Even our caving team from Kunming, usually more familiar with inland underground work, became underwater experts at diving in shallow water. Bill and Camilla are both working hard at diving to come up with as many new species as possible, identifying and checking every observation with fish books they brought along. They would make three or more dives each day.

跟 Camilla 很認真的潛水，希望可以找到許多新的物種，辨識牠們，也把書上的魚跟海裡的魚做交叉比對。他們一天至少潛個三次。

我個人沒有特別喜歡浮潛，這項運動對我來說還算新鮮，但是我也忍不住一天會下去潛個一兩次。有一天下午有兩尾小丑魚在我身邊待了快十五分鐘，我的心是滿滿的。其中一尾不捨得離開，還往我的潛水鏡裡探。當我在一個美麗的珊瑚上待著時，我突然想到我是不是觸犯到牠們的領域。也許這一對魚的小孩們正在我的下方關注我的一舉一動。

我在這裡停留，徘徊，因為我找到我的尼莫，牠不是在雪梨牙醫師診所裡的水族箱，而是在菲律賓巴拉望溫暖又潔淨的海水裡。

señorita / 那尾「小姐」

Though I am not particularly keen on snorkeling, being a new hand at the sport, I could not refuse diving in at least once or twice a day. The snap shots at times were quite rewarding, especially during one afternoon when two Anemonefish stayed with me for the better part of fifteen minutes. One of them simply refused to go away and peeked closely into my goggle. While I stayed put above a particularly beautiful coral, I finally realized that I must be infringing on their territory. Perhaps the couple was raising their young below me.

I lingered as long as I could, as here I found my Nemo, not in a dentist fish tank in Sydney, but in the warm and pristine water of Palawan in the Philippines.

writing 文字／ HM Wong 黃效文　photograph 攝影／ Li Na 李娜

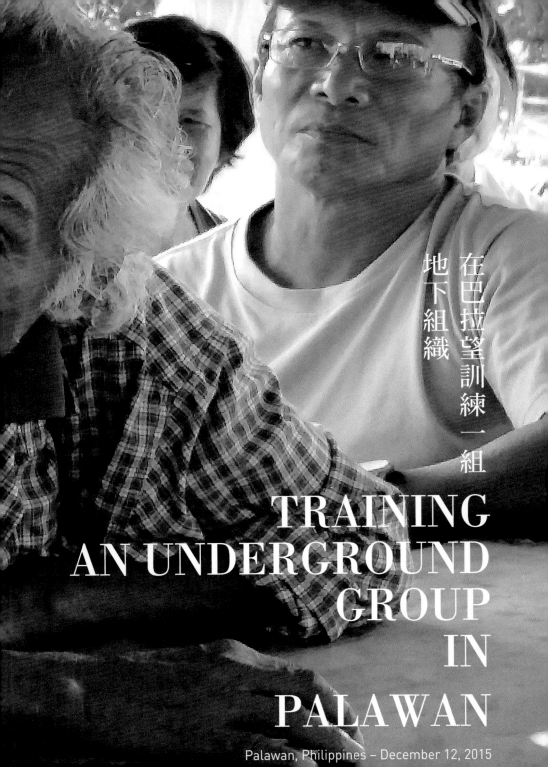

在巴拉望訓練一組
地下組織

TRAINING
AN UNDERGROUND
GROUP
IN
PALAWAN

Palawan, Philippines – December 12, 2015

在巴拉望訓練一組地下組織

正當中國與菲律賓為了南沙群島不停的以政治語言交鋒的同時，一群從中國雲南來的探洞隊伍正抵達巴拉望，來訓練這裡的地下軍隊一他們全部都是菲律賓村民；那備受爭議的島嶼就位於巴拉望的西邊。

偏遠的村莊跟一大片的溶岩石灰石互相依偎著，地底下藏著深淵與通道。這裡的青年不久後會開始帶領觀光客進入迷宮般的地洞參觀，這是屬於村莊的地洞，離世界遺產地底河流只有二十分鐘。

Palawan, Philippines – December 12, 2015

TRAINING AN UNDERGROUND GROUP
IN PALAWAN

While political rhetoric was flying through the air between China and the Philippines regarding the hotly contested Spratly Islands off the west coast of Palawan Island, a group of Chinese cavers from Yunnan arrived there to train an underground army, all Filipino villagers.

A remote village was nestled in an extensive landscape of karst limestone hills above ground, with abysses and passages below. Young members of this secluded community would soon begin leading tourists into a labyrinth of caves that belonged to their village, just twenty minutes from the World Heritage site of the Underground River.

The Yunnan group was part of the CERS Caving Team, led by Professor Zhang Fan who has been a scientific caver, or speleologist, since 1988. They first arrived in Palawan in May of 2015 and, with the guidance of a bird's nest collector and some intrepid villagers, entered the Hundred Caves and nearby Dinosaur Cave, both owned and managed by the village of Tagabinit with some 78 household members.

CERS caver teaching locals / CERS 探洞團隊教導當地人

125

CERS team lead the way / CERS 帶隊進入洞穴

雲南的團隊是 CERS 的探洞組，由張帆教授帶領，他是位
科學探洞家又可稱為洞窟學者，從 1988 年開始他的探洞
生涯。他們第一次抵達巴拉望是在 2015 年的五月，在採
燕窩者和幾位當地勇猛的村民陪伴下進入百洞穴跟旁邊的
恐龍洞穴，這兩個都是由馬蘭（Tagabinit）村民所擁有跟
管理的，全村大約有七十八人。

這一次 CERS 成功地為這兩個洞穴製作地圖，也製作了科
學的圖表，用來當作這兩個洞穴未來發展的基礎；一個洞

On that trip, the CERS team successfully mapped both caves, and later produced scientific charts which would form the basis of the development of the two cave systems, one into a tourist destination and the other with potential for slightly more technical exploration experience.

In this and a previous trip, the team explained the etiquette of professional caving, as well as experience gained in more advanced countries in the development of their caves for scientific studies, tourism and other commercial activities.

The team also provided training to the locals regarding special features that may be of interest to tourists, who might be fascinated by the karst formation underground. Conservation and protection issues were discussed, in order to prevent visitors from damaging the formation inside the caves. Safety issues were also included in the training program. CERS is also providing the local team with caving lights, helmets and future uniform.

While Palawan is filled with limestone hills and caves, their exploration and development for sustainable use is only at an infant stage. It is expected that, in years to come, opening caves to tourism will bring additional attraction and income to a pristine and yet unspoiled region of the Philippines.

As Henry Kissinger famously said, "there are no permanent enemies, only permanent interests". This effort between a CERS team from China and a

穴會開發成觀光景點，另一個有機會成為需要有點技術的探險體驗。

在這兩次的訪談中，我與團隊討論到專業探洞的理論，當然也討論到先進國家探洞的科學研究是怎麼做的，包括研究科學、觀光跟其他商業行為。

我們的團隊也提供專業的知識給當地人，例如地底下岩溶的形成，或許有些觀光客會對此感到興趣。關於保存與保護的議題也被討論到，像是怎麼避免觀光客破壞洞穴。關於安全的議題也包括在訓練的課程裡。CERS 也提供探洞用的燈、安全帽跟未來會用到的制服給當地的團隊。

即便巴拉望擁有豐富的石灰岩山丘和地洞，但是他們對這項資源的研究跟未來可以永續發展的經營模式還停留在初期階段。預計在未來，開放觀光客參觀洞穴會帶給菲律賓這個潔淨，尚未受汙染的地區一筆額外的收入。

季辛吉有句名言說，「沒有永遠的敵人，只有永遠的利益」。從中國來的 CERS 與菲律賓的團隊將一起證明，友誼與合作可以超越眼前短暫的不安與困難。

記得我是這樣告訴從香港出發來的團隊，「你們是要去巴拉望，不是派來玩」。很欣慰他們完成了我們為這計畫所設定的目標。

local Filipino group is a demonstration of friendship and cooperation that will transcend a temporary unfortunate and difficult time.

I remember telling my team when they embarked from Hong Kong, "You are going to Palawan, not Pailaiwan." (派來玩) The latter means sent to play. I am pleased that they have completed what we set out to achieve.

Homemade caving light / 自製探洞頭燈

離台灣最遠的外島

OUTERMOST ISLAND OF TAIWAN

Matsu, Taiwan – January 5, 2016

離台灣最遠的外島

這趟飛行，航空公司肯定是要虧錢的，要嘛，受政府補貼。全新的 *ATR pro-jet* 七十二人座，上面只有八位乘客，但有四位空服人員，包括兩位飛行員，乘客與工作人員形成二比一的比例。他們告訴我現在是淡季，在六、七月的時候會有很多來自台灣、香港還有中國大陸的觀光客。

飛一趟要四十五分鐘，氣候變化很大。我離開台北的時候還在下雨，到北竿時太陽很大。飯店老闆告訴我今年冬天異常的溫暖，但是晚上天氣會變差。我一點也不擔心，因為我準備的衣服可以讓我洋蔥式的穿脫。待會兒我會騎著摩托車出去逛逛，從這小島跳到另一個小島。簡單來說這裡有三個小島，北竿，南竿，東引。

小島上沒有麥當勞但是有 7-11。我的第一站北竿，大約有兩千多居民，這裡離大陸福建省開船只需要二十分鐘。有些居民在民宿工作，那是只有在夏天旅遊旺季才有的工作。這裡唯一一家 7-11 是大家最常去的咖啡店，一般民眾跟軍人都會來這裡，但不是買東西，而是來這裡喝

OUTERMOST ISLANDS OFF TAIWAN

My flight is subsidized. It has to be. For a new ATR prop-jet with 72 seats, there were only eight of us passengers. Four in the crew, including two pilots, provided a ratio of 2:1 in service. This is off-season. I was told that during June and July, many tourists arrive, from Taiwan, Hong Kong and Mainland China.

The flight took 45 minutes, but the weather is drastically different. It was raining when I left Taipei and here at Beigan the sun is shining. The owner of the hotel I stay told me that this year's winter has been exceptionally warm, and that the weather would change for the worse tonight. I am not worried a bit, as I have packed multiple layers of clothes, preparing for the worst. After all, I'll be scootering around hopping from island to island. In short, three islands in a nearby group, Beigan, Nangan, and Dongyin.

While there is no Big Mac being served on these islands, there are 7-Eleven's. My first stop is Beigan, an island only twenty minutes by boat from Mainland's Fujian Province, with slightly over 2000 inhabitants. Some residents are seasonal, working at home-stay hostels during the high season in

杯咖啡吃吃點心。

村裡只有幾條街道，還有幾家專門賣魚肉做的魚麵。負責的女士告訴我除了馬祖酒之外，這種麵也很受到觀光客的歡迎，還可以當作禮物。我看到街角有一間店，已經關了許久，老舊的招牌上面寫著建材，賣的建材像是切好的石頭，是用來蓋傳統房屋的那種。如今已經沒有人蓋這種房子了。

我待的芹壁村以前有超過一百棟也是用石頭蓋的房子，但現在不少都毀了。這幾十年來許多村民都到台北工作，留下來的沒幾戶。觀光客倒是比較喜歡住在這種傳統的房子裡，因此許多傳統的房屋被整修的很好，用來當作民宿或是精品住宿，有些整理的甚至比以前還漂亮。因為新的工作機會，也讓原本的居民漸漸回流，陳坤漢（Chen Kung-han）跟他的太太和兩個女兒就是這樣。住在他們那裏很愉快。

多年前留下來的政治軍事標語成為芹壁村房子的特色，水泥做的標語被刻在每家屋子的牆上。來自中國大陸跟台灣的觀光客覺得這些話很有趣，像是要大家效忠蔣介石，消滅叛徒毛氏與朱氏。還有標語寫著要消滅匪諜，光復大陸國土。

許多觀光客會去逛軍事設施，防禦陣地，這些我都跳過，

the summer. Here the only 7-Eleven store becomes also the most frequented café, with both civilians and soldiers stopping by not only to shop, but for a cup of coffee or a snack.

The village town has only a couple streets. A few shops specialized in making noodles from ground-up fish. The lady in charge told me that such noodles has become the most popular gift visitors would take home, besides the somewhat famous Matsu liquor. I saw a shop at the corner of one street. Long closed down, the old sign said it sells building material, meaning quarried boulder chiseled into rock pieces for the construction of traditional houses. Today no more houses are built in the old style.

Political slogan / 早期的宣傳口號

因為這裡跟我去年去的金門很像。我反而很喜歡這裡的風
景，尤其騎著摩托車，吹著微風的感覺更是奔放。

從我房外石砌的陽台往底下的海灘看，有個小石島在旁
邊，像隻靜止在水裡的烏龜，那正是這個小島的名字。流
浪貓和家貓到處遊走，難怪芹壁村會自傲的說這裡是台灣
的地中海。有些殘破房屋的牆面，破露出大小不同的石
頭，讓我想到四十年前在一九七五年去拜訪的馬丘比丘。

下一站是更南一點的南竿，開船只要十五分鐘。在碼頭辦
理住宿後我開始找摩托車。這個離島上還有好多蔣介石的
銅像，通常擺在圓環或是重要的地點。到處都是軍事偽

Madame café / 夫人咖啡一景

At the village I stayed, Chinbe, there used to be over a hundred households. Their houses, many of them in ruins, were all built with rocks cut from boulders in the area. Over the last few decades, most villagers had left for work in Taipei and only a few families remained. Today a new wave of tourists prefers to stay in traditional houses. Thus many such houses had been restored, some more beautiful than before, serving as home-stay or boutique hostels. The former residents are gradually returning, given the new opportunity. Chen Kung-han, his wife and their two daughters, are one such example. My stay with them was most pleasant.

A most significant feature of the houses at Chinbe is the political and military propaganda from decades ago. These cement slogans were engraved to the walls of each of the houses. Mainland as well as Taiwan tourist found such writings most appealing, from hailing loyalty and allegiance to Chiang Kai-shek, to destroying traitors Chu and Mao. One reminded everyone to get rid of bandit spies, and another proclaimed that the Mainland would soon be liberated.

While many tourists come to visit the numerous military installations and defense positions around the island, I skipped over all such attractions, finding the story and display rather repetitive after an earlier visit to Kinmen last year. Instead I rejoiced over the sceneries around the island, especially the liberating feeling of riding a motor scooter and catching the breeze.

裝，訴說著那個台灣與中國大陸互相敵對的年代。那年代早已被人遺忘，從對岸來的觀光財繼續注入這裡。

媽祖廟是台灣最受歡迎的廟，尤其是在離島。相傳媽祖為了救溺水的父親跳進海裡，祂保佑出海的人，特別是沿海的漁夫們。在南竿，有間古老的廟被重建，蓋的規模很大。旁邊的海軍登陸艇也成為海灘上的景點。

偏遠的村莊裡，有塊木製的招牌引發我的想像：夫人咖啡館。咖啡館坐落在山丘上，對著潔淨的海灘與海岸。我停下來，走下石階去喝杯咖啡。夫人不在，但是一位年輕的葉小姐在服務客人。她告訴我應該六月或七月再回來，那時候會有一種特別的海草，在夜晚海水拍打岩石的時候，會將海岸變成螢光藍。當地人稱這現象為「藍色的眼淚」。也許下次來的時候夫人也會在。

下一站東引。我不知道船的時間表已經改了，若我搭上了這艘船的話，我會被困在島上兩天，但我一定得趕回香港接待我的客人。就當遊輪正在收起讓車輛上下的木板時，我剛好發現這件事，他們將木板再放下讓我下船。

現在看起來我有個很好的理由再回來，也想像著夫人在咖啡館裡的樣子。在現今的社會裡，想像應該會比現實來的美好。所以我可以繼續在我的夢裡想著東引與夫人！

From the rock veranda outside my room, I looked down at the beach below and saw a nearby rock island. Perching above the calm water like a turtle, that is exactly what the island is called. Stray and domestic cats roamed around. No doubt Chinbe boasted that it is the Mediterranean of Taiwan. Some dilapidated houses have walls made from various sizes of rocks, reminding me of those at Machu Picchu that I visited in 1975.

My next stop was Nangan Island, a short hop of 15 minutes boat ride to the south. After checking into my hotel by the pier, I again took a scooter to explore the island. These off-shore islands still retain many statues of Chiang Kaishek, usually at roundabouts or positions of strategic importance. Camouflaged fortifications are everywhere, memory of decades past when Taiwan and the Mainland were hostile enemies against each other. Those days are now long forgotten, and tourist dollars are pouring in from across the strait.

The Matsu Temples are favorite of Taiwan, particularly so for the off-shore islands. The female goddess derived from a legend about a pious daughter plunging into the ocean to try saving her drowning father. Her spirit is supposed to bless all those going out to sea, in particular fishermen along the coast. At Nangan, the ancient temple now is totally rebuilt into a very large and elaborate massive. Nearby, navy landing craft on the beach became tourist site.

Chinbe village / 俯瞰芹壁村

At a remote hamlet, a wooden sign caught my imagination. "Fu Ren Café", meaning Madame Café, stood along a hillside overlooking a pristine beach and seacoast. I stopped and paced down the stone steps to have a cup of coffee. Madame was not in, but a young lady Miss Yeh was on hand to serve guests. She told me I should return in June or July, when a special type of seaweed would turn the coastline florescent blue at night when the waves pound the rocks. Locals called this phenomenon "Blue Teardrops". By then perhaps Madame would also be back.

My next stop should have been the island of Dongyin. But the boat schedule has changed without my knowledge, which would get me stranded on that island for two days. Whereas I must get back to Hong Kong in order to host a group of guests. Just as the cruise ship was lifting the vehicular plank to pull off, I discovered just in time and they lowered the plank in order for me to get off.

So now it seems I have a good reason to return, while fantasizing what Madame at the café may look like. As with much in this world today, the fantasy would portray something far more beautiful than in reality. So may I continue with my dream, both for Dongyin and for Madame!

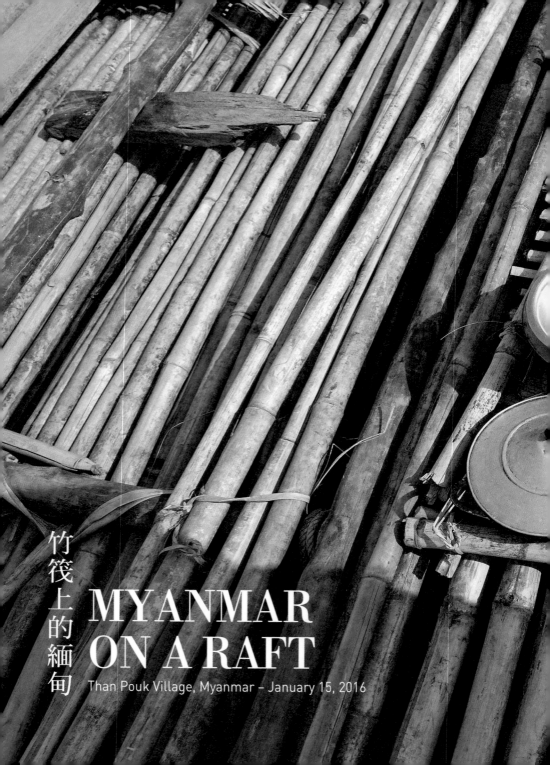

竹筏上的緬甸

MYANMAR
ON A RAFT

Than Pouk Village, Myanmar – January 15, 2016

竹筏上的緬甸

「對女人來說，最辛苦的事就是生小孩。對男人來說，最辛苦是在竹筏上工作，」*Daw Nyein* 告訴我這個古老的緬甸名言。對她來說這兩件事都是辛苦的事，因為她都做過，生過一個小孩，也在竹筏上工作過。竹筏上的工作是暫時的，只有幾年。但是養小孩是一輩子的，她兒子快要從蒙育瓦（*Monywa*）大學畢業了。她接下來的願望就是為兒子找到一個好老婆，讓她有個好媳婦。

很少人會喜歡在竹筏上工作，但是 *Daw Nyein* 一邊露出滿意的微笑一邊跟我們在竹筏上聊天，竹筏大概有一個籃球場那麼大。她微笑，因為她現在這件辛苦的事可以扶養二十三年前她開始的另一項辛苦的事。

自從兒子 *Aung Ko Latt* 讀完十一年級，到高中，到進大學，*Daw Nyein* 跟丈夫 *Kyaw* 一起在竹筏上工作已經長達六年了；一年有三次他們得從卡列瓦到蒙育瓦的下游織組一艘竹筏要花四個月的時間，即使是小竹筏也要用上五千根竹子，從卡列瓦漂流到市場需要花上約一個禮拜。在沒有小

MYANMAR ON A RAFT

"For a woman, the hardest work is giving birth to a child. For a man, the hardest work is to be on a raft". Daw Nyein told me this old Burmese saying. Surely for her, it is by far the hardest, as she has done both, giving birth to a child and working on a raft. Working the raft may be temporary, only for a few years. But raising a child seems permanent, though her son is now finishing graduate school at Monywa University. Her next big wish is that he would find a perfect wife, or for her, a daughter-in-law.

Few would find working a raft so gratifying, as a contended smile readily came to Daw Nyein's face when we chatted on their bamboo raft, a raft about the size of a basketball court. It is because she is doing one hardest job in order to support the other hardest job she brought to life 23 years ago.

For six years, since their son Aung Ko Latt finished 11th grade, then through college and now in graduate school, she and her husband Kyaw Than have been working a raft downriver from Kalewa to Monywa three times a year. It takes four months to assemble a raft, considered small in size using 5,000 bamboos. This is followed by about a week to float down the river from

馬達的時候，這趟旅程要花上十天到兩周。夏天雨季的時候，水流湍急，得花上更多時間，因為河道會出現彎曲的危險地帶。

他們付了訂金，一根竹子兩百 *Kyat*（一美金約八百 *Kyat*），付了訂金才有竹子可以組船。有些竹筏是四倍大，需要兩萬根竹子。旅途的另一端，一根竹子要兩百三十 *Kyat*。如果沒有意外的話，每趟他們可以賺六萬到十萬 *Kyat*。

Daw Nyein 一提到她兒子 *Aung Ko Latt*，就馬上跑進棚子找兒子的學生證給我們看。我們在一個叫做 *Kyi Taung Oo*

Kalewa to market. In the past, without the small motor, the journey may take ten days to two weeks. During the rainy season in the summer when the current is fast, it may take a few days longer than a week, rather than faster, to negotiate the dangerous bends on the river.

They paid a deposit, based on a price of 200 Kyat (US$1 equals 800 Kyat) per bamboo, before assembling the raft. Some rafts may be up to four times the size of hers, with up to 20,000 bamboos. At the other end of the trip, each bamboo would be sold for 230 Kyat. Each trip may earn them between 60,000 to 100,000 Kyat in profit; that is, if there are not too many surprise charges along the way.

Once Daw Nyein mentioned her son Aung Ko Latt, she quickly rushed inside her shed and brought out her son's student ID with a picture to show off. We are stopping off at the village of Kyi Taung Oo where several bamboo rafts are mooring to the bank of the Chindwin River. Daw Nyein is hopeful that in three more days, she may arrive Monywa and see her son. He has finished all his studies and is waiting for the graduation ceremony to take place. The parents, proud parents, are also waiting to attend.

But for now, they, as well as the other rafters, are stranded. Not by the many sandbars on the river during dry season, but by the local authority. Day and night, police along such villages would stop the rafts and extort a fee, or a fine

in name, from these poor rafters, before allowing them to continue with their journey. Hopefully this unscheduled, but to be expected, stop would not last too long once they can negotiate the asking price of 50,000 kyats down to something more reasonable and affordable. Today, they may not be able to negotiate too hard, given her urge to see her son.

But for her son Aung Ko Latt, he may have to remain philosophical with his new degree of Master in Philosophy. For him, finding a wife may be easier than finding a job, a good job. This can be demonstrated by 30-years-old Ko Thar Lin Oo, another graduate of Monywa University, with a degree in Law. Today, he is working a raft, slightly larger with 7,000 bamboos, heading down river toward the same destiny, that of an uncertain future.

While a new Myanmar seems to be full of hope and dreams, some may materialize, others unfulfilled. For the rafters, situation has gotten worse. But they hope it would get better once the new government is installed following a landslide election victory by the opposition.

的村莊暫時停留，看見好幾艘載竹子的竹筏停靠在欽敦江的岸邊。*Daw Nyein* 很開心，因為再過三天就能抵達蒙育瓦，也就可以見到兒子了。他已經完成他的學業正等待著畢業典禮，而父母，驕傲的父母也一樣的在等待著。

不過現在所有的竹筏都被困住。不是被枯竭的河水，而是被當地政府。不管是白天還是黑夜，警察都會跟村民勒索，開罰單，之後才會放行。希望這個不在行程裡的事（但可預期），不會耽誤太久。討價還價後，省了五萬 *Kyats*，至少合理點，也是個比較可以負擔的價錢。今天他們不能很強硬討價，因為趕著要去看兒子。

她的兒子 *Aung Ko Latt* 也許需要用哲學的態度去看待他的哲學系畢業證書。對他來說找個好老婆可能比找個好工作更容易。這點三十歲的 *Ko Thar Lin Oo* 可以證明，他也是畢業於蒙育瓦大學的法律系。如今他還是在竹筏上工作，一艘七千多根竹子的竹筏，正往下游去，去到一個未知的未來。

新的緬甸看起來好像充滿希望與夢想，有些可能實現，有些可能不會。對竹筏工人來說，狀況只有變得更糟。但是他們希望新的政府上任後情況會好轉，反對黨這次壓倒性的贏得選舉的勝利。

For Ko Thar Lin Oo, his journey started at Homalin further upriver, and it would require 16 days minimum to arrive at Ahlone, a point slightly above Monywa where the bamboos are sold to wholesalers. His bamboos are however of better quality, costing 250 to 300 Kyats each, and sold for 500 at market. Bamboo rafting has been his family's business. At their hometown, it takes seven years for a bamboo grove to grow to size for harvest.

When asked about the profit he makes, Ko Thar put on a grim face. "I'll be lucky if I break even on this trip," he answered. So far he has been stopped ten times since leaving Homalin. Each of these stops are by the local forestry "police", extorting a fine, or a fee to keep a blind eye, to let the raft through the section of the river under their jurisdiction. None of these fines come with a receipt. At times, they have to literally beg the authority for a smaller fee such that they can still earn the little they can. And in the three days ahead, there are several more gates to cross.

The next raft we stopped provided even a grimmer story. Forty years old Ko Win Htay is the "boss" of this raft. As such, his loss on this trip will be solely born by him, rather than his hired hands on the raft, a timber raft. He was carrying, or floating, teak log harvested from near his home village of Yay Sa Kyo Village in Pakhok Ku township. Teak cutting is strictly regulated, with concessions given to favored timber baron whereas for common people totally restricted. He needed to pay a larger fine to get his cargo through the many

Ko That Lin Oo 的旅程從霍馬林（*Homalin*）上游開始，
到阿弄區（*Ahlone*）最少要花上十六天，阿弄區在蒙育瓦
的北邊一點點，批發商會來這裡批竹子。他的竹子品質
比較好，一根要二百五十到三百 *Kyat*，賣到市場要五百
Kyat。竹筏是他的家族事業。在家鄉，種植一片竹林到可
以採收需要七年的時間。

當被問到可以賺多少錢時，*Ko That* 的臉垮了下來。「我
這趟如果可以打平的話就很幸運了！」他回答。從霍馬林
開始到目前為止，他已經被攔下來十次了。當地森林「警
察」攔他下來要求勒索罰款，如果乖乖照做，警察就會裝
作甚麼都沒看見的讓他們通過。這些罰款都沒有收據，有
時候他們還必須跟做官的乞求罰少一點，讓他們至少可以
有一點點賺頭。未來的三天還有更多的河閘要過呢。

後來遇到的竹筏告訴了我們更嚴峻的故事。四十歲的 *Ko
Win Htay* 是這艘竹筏的「老闆」。正因如此，這趟的損
失都算他的，而不是他雇用的工人，這是艘載木材的竹
筏。他載的柚木原木是從他家鄉附近的小村子 *Yay Sa Kyo*
砍的，*Yay Sa Kyo* 位在 *Pakhok Ku* 區。伐柚木的規定很嚴
格，伐木的權利通常都是屬於筏木大亨，平常人是沒有機
會碰的。所以他必須在每個檢查站付大筆的罰金才有辦法
運送他的貨品。

river check points.

Harvesting teak, hauling them to the river, assembling them as a raft, takes far more time and exerted greater energy. That alone would require up to six months. But the profit is supposed to be more lucrative, if delivered to market without too many stops. When asked how many stops he made to pay fine, Ko Win Htay felt disgusted to count, and simply said, "One hundred stops!" After all, he has been away from his family for six months already, and with

砍伐柚木後，將它們拖到河裡，再組裝成一艘木筏，是一件耗時耗力的事。這件事要花上六個月的時間。利潤應該相當可觀，如果運到市場的旅程裡沒有被攔下來太多次的話。當我們問到他被攔下來幾次，*Ko Win Htay* 想到就生氣，他回說「一百次！」。畢竟他已經離家六個月了，口袋還是空空，家似乎還很遠。

新的緬甸開始建設基礎設施跟交通，這個安靜，步調緩慢的國家正在改變中。遲早現代化將會取代舊有旅行的方式，像是河裡的竹筏。對竹筏船夫這樣肆意的、貪婪的「開罰」，估計很快的令竹筏也將會消失，消失在朦朧裡，像清晨欽敦江上的霧。

his pockets still empty, home seems far away.

With a new Myanmar, modern infrastructure and transportation are gradually being put in place, transforming a once quiet and slow country. It is only a matter of time such modernization will replace old method of travels, like rafting on the river. But with the arbitrary and insatiable "fine" to the rafters, such historical tradition may die a sooner death, fading into obscurity like the morning mist over the Chindwin River.

從後門的後門進入緬甸

BACK BACK DOOR INTO MYANMAR

Border Post 41 China/Myanmar – February 9, 2016

從後門的後門進入緬甸

「*Sa Khan*」身穿紅色襯衫緬甸長裙的年輕小姐說。「請你再說一遍」我麻煩她,因為我試圖記錄下正確的發音。「*Sa Khan*」她又說了一遍,因為邊境貿易的關係,其實這位小姐是會說幾句中文的。王健很認真地用筆記本把字的發音記下來,把名字搞對是很重要的一件事。

我正處在緬甸最偏遠的地方,這裡靠近中國的邊境,鄰近雲南跟西藏,非常的偏遠。兩年前只有在中國國境那邊才有土石路;而在緬甸這邊,只有一條小徑,藉著它穿過叢林後才能來到三公里外的第一個鄉鎮。

從中國邊境的邊防標示「*41*號界碑」回來,發了簡訊給我在緬甸的區域經理,我才知道她說的是「崗哨」。我們拜訪的這間屋子外懸掛著緬甸國旗,走過很危險的路,費了很大的勁,我們才來到這裡。這真的可以說是緬甸後門的後門。

儘管我們有許多研究跟保育的項目在緬甸,大家比較不知

BACK BACK DOOR INTO MYANMAR

"Sa Khan," said the young lady in a red blouse and Burmese Longyi skirt. "Again please?" I requested, trying to record the phonetic pronunciation accurately. "Sa Khan," she said once again. The lady spoke a few simple words of Chinese, due perhaps to the trickle of border trade coming through. Wang Jian dutifully scripted down the sound of the word in his notebook. It is important to get the name right.

Here I am at the remotest corner of Myanmar bordering China, edging on Yunnan and Tibet. So remote that only two years ago a dirt road on the Chinese side reached the border. On the Myanmar side, even today only a marginal footpath penetrates the jungle leading to the first settlement some three kilometers away.

Later I was to find out the name means simply "station" or "sentry", after I returned to Border Post 41 on the China side and texted my Myanmar Country Manager. There was a Myanmar national flag outside the house we visited. We had come a long way to get here, through a most hazardous path. Literally, this can be considered a back back door into Myanmar.

道的是我有好幾次從後門進入緬甸的經驗。多年來我用合法，非法，或是半合法的各種方式進入緬甸。二零零九年我從盈江縣進入最近戰亂的 Lazie 鎮，這個小鎮被 KIA（克欽獨立軍）反政府分子所佔領。我們一路進到密支那，一個由政府掌控的北方城市。我們一共有八個人用「邊境」居民的身份進入，當然這都是有文件可以證明的。

二零零零年的時候我穿過騰衝邊境城鎮的 Dietan，進入由 KNDF 叛軍（克欽新民主前線）掌控的伐木區，他們看似共產黨。我在這裡拜訪傈僳族住所跟他們的教堂。這裡的傈僳族源自於雲南，在一九八零年代中國政府對於他們的宗教強加限制，所以他們跨過邊境來到這裡。估計大約有百分之三十的傈僳族沿著漫長的薩爾溫江跨境移居到緬甸。

最有趣的是在二零零六年，十年前，我從地底下進入緬甸，洞穴的入口在中國的鎮康縣，出口在緬甸。邊防標示 124 界碑就在我們頭上。除了隱密的洞口之外，在中國這邊到處都有檢查站跟邊境守衛，緬甸那邊也到處都是哨兵。

但是這次我是從一個大家不知道的地方進入緬甸的。首先我從未想過這裡會沒有邊境的檢查站跟邊境守衛，也沒有移民官或是海關，邊境的兩邊都沒有。這條路非常危險，有些地方只有鋪著一根樹幹，陡峭岩壁下的就是獨龍江，

Beautifully treacherous / 危險卻又美麗

Despite our many research and conservation projects in Myanmar, less well known to others are the several times I entered the country through the backdoor. Over the years, I have entered Myanmar, legally, illegally, or paralegally. In 2009, I entered through Yingjiang County and into the recent war zone town of Lazai controlled by the KIA (Kachin Independent Army) insurgency. We went all the way to Myitkyina, a northern city controlled by the government. Eight of us in the team all posted as "border" residents with matching paperwork.

Hamlet with Myanmar flag / 矗立緬甸國旗的村落

Still earlier in 2000, I penetrated through Tengchong County's Dientan border town, into a logging region controlled by another insurgent army KNDF (Kachin New Democratic Front), a communist outfit, and visited a Lisu settlement and their chapel. These Lisu were offshoot of those in Yunnan, crossing the border in the 1980s when the Chinese government imposed restrictions on their religious practice. It was estimated that as many as 30% of the Lisu along the lengthy border of the Salween River may have crossed the border to resettle in Myanmar.

Perhaps most interesting was in 2006, ten years ago, when I entered through the underground, crossing from a cave of Zhenkang County with entrance on the China side and exited in Myanmar. This is where Border Sign Post 124 is marked above our heads. Except for the stealthy cave entry, there are always check points and border guards on the Chinese side, as well as Burmese sentry on the other side.

This time however I entered Myanmar through a totally unknown crossing. At first, I did not imagine such would be the case, no border check point, no border guard, no immigration nor customs, on both sides of the border. The foot path was so hazardous that at sections the access was by a single log crossing, with precipitous rock sides overhanging crevice below into the Dulongjiang, uppermost reaches of the Irrawaddy River.

依洛瓦底江的最上游。

有兩個地方我們都必須將身體貼著岩壁，小心翼翼地踩在一根樹幹上小步前進。雖身處在偏遠的地方，但如果在這裡不小心掉到獨龍江的話，便是到仰光的捷徑，只要下游兩千公里就到仰光。這條路需要爬上爬下，視乎你是從哪一個方向來的。有的路是用竹子做的階梯，搖晃得很厲害，有的路更陽春，幾乎是直立的樹幹兩旁用小木塊固定，這樹幹就成了階梯。

如此的旅程，如果可以稱得上 "旅程" 這兩個字的話，讓我又驚又喜。內心裡我像個小男孩在叢林裡攀爬，但是外在提醒了我是個膝蓋不好腳步又不穩的老人。還好內心的小男孩給了我足夠的動力去克服那個老人。儘管我的高齡，我還在尋找通往依洛瓦底江源頭的路，位於西藏的東南部，希望這個探險的行程今年可以成行。但是沿途我分心了，冒險橫過中國與緬甸的邊境。

從昆明開車要五天才能到這裡，然後要再爬三公里才可以進入到第一個緬甸的村落，這段是旅途的高潮。這個村落有一間兩層樓的房子是政府設的崗哨，三間茅草屋，第四間房子正在蓋，有六個村民正在為這房子立樑柱。

這些人是杜因族，在中國被稱作獨龍族。他們一直以來是

At two locations, we have to lean our body a bit sideways against the rock face, while gingerly inching forward in small steps to cross such single log. Remote as we were, there was a fast track to Yangon two thousand kilometers downriver, if one were to fall off into the Dulongjiang, fatality assured. There were also drops along the path, as well as climbs, depending which direction the person is coming from. Some were rickety bamboo ladder passages. Others were even simpler, an almost perpendicular log with small pieces of wood nailed sideways, serving as a makeshift ladder.

Such journey, if it could be called a journey, gave me both pleasure and trepidation. Internally, I derived the joy of a young boy climbing through the jungle, and externally caution as an aging man with weak knees and unsteady steps. Fortunately the former gave impetus to help overcome the latter. Despite my advancing age, I was scouting for a way to the Irrawaddy source in southeastern Tibet that we hope to explore later this year. But along the way, I got distracted and ventured across the China-Myanmar border.

From Kunming it took us five days of driving to get here. And now the last three kilometers hike across the border into Myanmar's first village was the high point of the trip. Besides a two-storied house serving as a government sentry, there were three other small thatch houses. A fourth one was just being constructed as the beams and posts were being raised by half a dozen villagers.

Myanmar Drung at home / 緬甸杜因族的家居生活

These people are the Drungs, or on the China side, the Dulong people. As traditional hunters of the forest, they live much like the Lisu except even more basic and primitive. The tattooed faces of the women could hardly be seen anymore as only the most senior ladies still sport such eclipsing tradition of the past. Just a day ago, I chanced upon one such lady as I watched an impromptu dance gathering at a village on the China side of the border. Today, China has fewer than 4,000 Dulong people among its minorities population.

This is only the Second Day of Chinese New Year, an auspiciously Losar New Year for the Tibetan living not too far away. A few young women were cooking on a massive wok inside the kitchen of one of the thatch houses. There were also around ten young children and infants around. As the rain was getting heavier, soon the young men building a new house started filing in.

I saw on the wall hung a weaved basket, a crossbow and a bamboo twin-barrel bamboo arrow holder. We negotiated to buy these to add to the CERS collection of ethnographic objects. Rain was getting heavier all the time and we must make it back across the border before night fell. Thus the offer went up higher and higher and the outside sky got dimmer and dimmer. Finally, the owner of the bow and arrow took on a more serious interest.

We left and headed back to China with our trophies. Inside the bamboo

森林裡的獵人，生活跟傈僳族很相像，只是更原始。紋面的女人已經幾乎找不到了，只有在年長婦女的臉上才能看到這傳統。而就在一天前我恰巧遇到一位這樣的婦人，那是在中國邊境村民的即興舞蹈聚會中。現在中國的獨龍族已經不到四千人了。

今天是中國新年的第二天，對住在不遠的西藏人來說也是個吉利的藏曆新年。茅草屋內，幾位年輕的女性正在廚房用一個很大的鍋子煮飯，大概有十個小孩跟幼兒在附近玩耍。雨越下越大，正在蓋房子的年輕人開始湧進屋子裡。

我看到牆上掛著一個編織的籃子、一個弩弓還有兩個裝竹箭用的竹桶。我們跟他們交涉購買這幾樣東西，為 CERS 的民族學添加收藏品。雨下的很大，我們為了要趕在天黑前回到邊境，隨著外面的天色越來越暗，價錢也出的越來越高。最後弓箭的主人終於同意賣給我們。

帶著戰利品往中國的方向前進。竹桶內有兩打竹箭，每支的箭頭都塗抹著用當地植物提煉的劇毒，這種箭是用來獵大型動物的。在回去的路上，我一直在想回家後該怎麼測試這些毒箭才好。

大約過了一個鐘頭我們回到 41 界碑的邊境，我們決定在附近紮營。晚餐正在爐火上煮著，我發現我 iPhone 上面

Turquoise river water / 碧綠色的河水

container were two dozen arrows. Each head of these arrows was tinted with a most viral poison made from a potent local plant. They were used to hunt for big game. During our hike back, it weighed heavily on my mind how to test them when I get home.

After another hour or so, we arrived back at Border Post 41. We decided to set our camp a short distance from the post. While cooking our dinner over a stove, I suddenly noticed that my iPhone was behind in time for an hour and a half. It was registering Myanmar rather than China time!

的時間遲了一個半鐘頭，它顯示的是緬甸的時間而不是中國的時間！

帳篷外的氣溫很低，我思考著是否應該要相信現代的科技，包括我的 *iPhone* 上面 *GPS* 的邊境分界數據，還是應該要相信近六十年前，一九六零年立的標示。我們到底是在緬甸紮營還是在中國？像在邊境穿梭的動物，突然間這問題顯得很無關也輕浮，尤其跟另一個問題相比：我的睡袋不知道可不可以讓我度過這零下的夜晚！

With freezing weather outside our tent, I contemplated whether I should put my trust in modern technology, including the GPS reading I have on my iPad, or should I believe in a sign post erected almost 60 years ago, in 1960. Are we camping in Myanmar or China? Like the animals crossing back and forth, suddenly it all seemed quite irrelevant and frivolous, compared to whether my sleeping bag would bear me through the night in this sub-zero weather!

Tattooed Dulong woman / 紋面的杜因族婦人

見到新種金絲猴的第一眼

YEAR OF THE MONKEY

Pienma, Yunnan – February 11, 2016

猴年——見到新種金絲猴的第一眼

在二十一世紀想要發現新的物種是件難事，更別說是哺乳動物。要找到跟鑑定靈長類動物幾乎不可能，不過它確實發生了。

二零一零年十月七日，*BBC* 首次報導在緬甸北部發現新種的猴子。目前所知道的是，緬甸的這種是金絲猴的第五種，也可能是最後一個在世界上被發現的金絲猴（正確的學名是塌鼻猴）種類。這個新聞很快的成為頭條。

CERS 團隊對這則新聞感到特別興奮，因為我們很多人參與雲南金絲猴項目很多年了。對畢博士來說更是如此，因為他觀察及研究其它四個種類的金絲猴有好一段時間了，在四川（第一次發現是在一八七零年）、雲南（一八九七年）、貴州（一九零三年），甚至在越南北部（一九一二年）。

將近一世紀前，最後一個金絲猴的種類被國際動植物組織（*FFI*）發現。畢博士曾經是這組織在中國的主任，他覺

YEAR OF THE MONKEY
– first look at a new monkey species

For the 21st Century, it is hard enough to find a new species, harder yet to find a new mammal, and next to impossible to find and identify a new primate. But that is exactly the case.

On October 27, 2010, BBC broke the news that a new species of monkey was discovered in northern Myanmar. Now known as the Burmese, or Myanmar, Snub-nosed Monkey, it is the fifth and perhaps the last species of Snubnosed Monkey to be discovered in the world. Soon the news hit headlines all over the world.

Those of us at CERS took the news with much more excitement, as many of us have been working closely with the Yunnan Snub-nosed Monkey over the years. For Bill Bleisch, it was more than excitement as he has observed all four of the other species of Snub-nosed Monkey, in Sichuan (first discovered in 1870), Yunnan (1897), Guizhou (1903) and even northern Vietnam (1912).

Almost a century after the last snub-nosed monkey was discovered, the new

Scratch scratch! / 抓癢！

species was discovered by Flora and Fauna International (FFI). Bill worked at one time as FFI's China Head, and thought perhaps there might be room for collaboration, and thus contacted his friends at FFI. Word soon came that FFI would not want anyone moving into the same area to work. Perhaps the American billionaire philanthropist Jon Stryker, who funded the survey, felt proprietary about the discovery. Indeed Rhinopithecus strykeri, the scientific Latin name assigned to this new species, bore the name of this gentleman from Michigan in the United States.

Thus we felt cut out of future research of this new, rare and endangered species. The identification of this species by FFI field scientists, however, was based on a dead animal, later eaten by the hunters. In survey and interviews of local Lisu hunters, they estimated between 260 to 300 animals remaining within Myanmar.

One dramatic story mentioned in the news was that these monkeys always lower their heads and cover their face when it rains. Otherwise the upturned nose catching raindrops would make them sneeze, thus revealing their position to predators and hunters. Bill has watched snub-nosed monkeys for more than 150 hours in the wild, including in driving rainstorms, and he tells me that he has never seen such behavior.

There have not been any clear pictures of the new Snub-nosed Monkey posted

得應該可以有合作的空間，於是跟在這組織裡的友人聯
絡。消息很快的傳回，FFI 不希望在這區有其他人也做同
樣的研究。美國的億萬富翁 Jon Stryker，也是個慈善家，
他資助這項研究，或許他覺得這是他的研究地盤。事實證
明，這一項新發現的命名是 Rhinopithecus strykeri，取自
這個美國密西根紳士的名字。

基於上述的原因，我們覺得應該沒有機會參與這瀕臨絕
種動物的研究了。事實上 FFI 田野科學家用來辨識這新
種類的猴子其實是隻死的，後來這隻還被獵人給吃掉了。
在調查與訪問傈僳族的獵人後，他們估計大概還有兩
百六十隻到三百隻的猴子還存在緬甸境內。

新聞報導裡比較戲劇性的說，這些猴子在下雨天的時候
會把頭放低，把臉遮起來。會把頭放低的原因是牠們的
朝天鼻進雨水的話牠們就會打噴嚏，這樣就會被掠奪者
跟獵人知道牠們所在的位置。畢博士在野外觀察金絲猴
已經超過一百五十個鐘頭，也曾在暴雨中觀察牠們，但
是他告訴我，他從沒看過猴子有這樣的行為。

網路上沒有任何一張清楚的新種類的金絲猴照片，只有
一張兩個當地人舉著一隻死掉的猴子，還有依照猴子的
頭骨跟皮膚去合成的影像，跟一些定點照相機拍到的模
糊照片。如果上網 Google 緬甸金絲猴，搜尋不到什麼東

online, except the dead animal held up by two locals, and composite images based on that animal or from skulls and skins, and some fuzzy images from camera traps. If one were to Google Burmese/Myanmar Snub-nosed Monkey images, not much would show up except many of the other species previously known. That however, would change soon, once I am to post up our images from this story.

Perhaps due to this being the Year of the Monkey, and merit of our restoring a meditation house of Damazong (Bodhidharma) who was born in India under the Monkey Zodiac and considered the first Patriarch Master Monk who brought Buddhism to China in the early 6th Century, we were graced by seeing this new monkey species. On my recent expedition to Yunnan bordering Tibet and Myanmar, while visiting an exhibit along the Salween River hosted by the local Tourism Bureau, a photograph caught my eyes. It was of this Myanmar Snub-nosed Monkey, very much like the Yunnan species except being Black in color.

My interest soon turned only to this picture. I was given the hint that the nearby Gaoligongshan has a live specimen within a reserve station. Soon telephones started ringing as I called my friends in key position and leadership within the conservation and nature reserve circle. The animal turned out to be three years old, a female, picked up as an infant by hunters when a group of these monkeys left in a hurry during a snowstorm. It was turned over to the

西，只有一些之前早已發現的種類的資料。不過這即將會
有改變，我將會把我們的照片放在網路上。

也許因為今年是猴年，還有我們修復了一間達摩祖師洞
閉關房子的原因，我們才有機會見到這個新種類的猴子。
達摩祖師出生於印度，猴年生，為中國禪宗第一代祖師，
在六世紀初將佛教帶入中國。最近一趟考察我去了雲南、
西藏跟緬甸的邊界，在薩爾溫江旁我們看了一個由當地
旅遊局主辦的展覽，展覽裡有張照片吸引了我的目光。
那是緬甸的金絲猴，跟雲南的金絲猴很像，只是緬甸的
是黑色的，也可算是黑絲猴吧。

我對這張照片非常感興趣。有人告訴我在附近的高黎貢
山自然保護區裡有一隻活的猴子。於是我馬上打電話給
在自然保育圈裡的重量級友人。這隻猴子三歲，母的，
暴風雪的時候猴子們急著逃離，當時幼小的牠沒跟上，
後來被獵人拾回，轉給了自然保護區。

很明顯的在中國的傈傈族，靠薩爾溫江西岸叢林這邊的
獵人早已知道這猴子的存在。但是這種猴子總是有辦法
閃躲掉所有的田野科學家跟靈長類動物學家。事實上最
早在二零一一年的十月，當地的保護區管理員曾經拍過
一群緬甸金絲猴。現在最少有六個猴群被確認，保護區
裡至少有六百隻，在中國境內這邊遊走。*CERS* 現在正在

nature reserve.

Obviously Lisu hunters on the China side along the west bank jungle of the Salween River have always known of its existence. However this new species has somehow eluded and evaded all field biologists and primatologists. In fact, as early as October 2011, a local reserve ranger had taken pictures of a sizable group of this Snub-nosed Monkey. Today, at least half a dozen groups have been identified, and the nature reserve estimated up to 600 animals may roam within China's border. CERS is now in the process to work out a plan to be involved in the study and protection of this new and exciting species.

It seems only natural that I would insist on paying a visit to befriend this beautiful female, a three-year-old Myanmar Snub-nosed Monkey. Though far away inside the nature reserve, our meeting was arranged. As far as I am concerned, this species' most likely home range and ancestral heritage must be in China, with some families straying/migrating into Myanmar. Our rendezvous, which was on the fourth day of Chinese New Year, seemed to set the stage for a most auspicious Year of the Monkey. With luck, we'll be back again later this year.

計畫參與這項研究，希望可以保育這個令人興奮的動物。

很自然地我覺得我應當去拜訪這位美麗的女性，三歲的緬甸金絲猴，雖然我們的會面被安排在保護區內很偏遠的地方。對我來說這種類的猴子應該是源自於中國，只是有些家族遊蕩進入緬甸。我們的會面是在中國新年的第四天，今年會是個吉祥的猴年。運氣好的話，今年我們還會再回來。

Yummy beans / 好吃的豆子

AGONY
AND ECSTASY

Kushiro, Hokkaido – February 29, 2016

痛苦與狂喜

痛苦與狂喜

冬天裡拍攝鶴與海鷹

中國人要來了！但是我也是中國人，我已經連續好多年都會來北海道，在寒冷的冬天住在同一個寧靜又質樸的家庭民宿裡。

今年有點不同。華人真的到了，從中國大陸、台灣、香港、新加坡、美國，幾乎是世界各地。透過網路大家都發現冬天的北海道有個拍照的好地方。來到這裡的華人，特別是從中國大陸來的，不少是暴發戶。以前出國旅行是屬於特定人士的權利，現在大多數的人都可以到處旅行了。

拿破崙的預言是對的！當中國醒來後，它會影響這世界。這個沉睡的巨人已經醒了，腳印踏進世界最偏遠的角落，他們去的已經不只是只跟商業利益有關的地方，也開始會去休閒的地方了。

我也醒了，從白日夢中醒了，一邊做夢一邊泡在釧路濕地溫度剛好的溫泉中。在我旁邊有一群在睡夢中的白天鵝，釧路湖這裡溫暖的水成為牠們冬天的家。牠們也醒了，就

Kushiro, Hokkaido – February 29, 2016

AGONY AND ECSTASY
Photographing crane and sea eagle in the winter

The Chinese are coming! But I am Chinese too, and I have been here in Hokkaido for many years, a peaceful and pristine retreat that has become my yearly ritual during winter.

Somehow this year is different. The Chinese have really arrived, from the Mainland, Taiwan, Hong Kong, Singapore, America, just about from everywhere. Through the internet, they have all discovered the photographic paradise of winter Hokkaido. And today the Chinese, especially those from the Mainland, are the nouveau riche. What was once considered the domain of the select few has now become available to many, many.

Napoleon's prophecy was right! When China wakes up, it will shake the world. And the Sleeping Giant has woken up, with footprint stomping into even some of the remotest corners of the world, not just economically with commercial interest, but also in leisure destinations.

I too, have woken up, from day-dreaming while soaking in the perfectly warm

當五個中國攝影師帶著長鏡頭和腳架來到這裡的時候。

今天早上只有我一個人在泡溫泉。過去幾年，我曾經看過日本女士男士會在這個靠湖的天然溫泉泡湯。現在溫泉旁有兩個英文牌子，上面寫著「禁止在此裸泳」。也許當地人覺得自己的聖地被入侵。因為來這裡攝影的人實在是太多了，有的鏡頭對準的還不只是天鵝！

就在這時候，兩個華人跨過竹籬笆，就在我前面拍起天鵝來。竹籬笆外面其實有很多隻天鵝，但是不知道為什麼他們覺得我在的那小塊地方比較吸引人。我很快的穿上衣服，決定離開這溫暖的、寒冬裡冒著白煙的溫泉。我的四周都是白雪，湖畔也都是雪。在兩輛載滿觀光客的巴士抵達前我趕快離開。下一個溫泉，更多的巴士，也同樣不是我會停的一站。

確實在過去多年，在寒冬中來到北海道是我每年必做的事，甚至是一種朝聖，身處在大自然中，有鶴，海鷹，鹿，狐狸作伴。我很喜歡拍野生動物，也很喜歡拍雪景。不是以一個職業的攝影師或是商業攝影師的身分，我單純的很享受一邊開車一邊停下拍照。我通常一天只開個兩個鐘頭，常常停下車，站在戶外享受寒冷的微風。一些我最喜歡的野生動物跟自然景觀的照片都是在下雪時的北海道拍的。

Sleeping swan / 睡眠中的天鵝

water of the Kussharogenya hot spring. Next to me is a flock of sleeping white swan, making the warm water of Lake Kussharo their winter home. They too were woken up, just as five Chinese photographers arrived at the scene, lugging their long lens cameras and tripods.

This morning, I am the only person in the hot spring. In years past, I have seen Japanese old ladies and men, soaking in this natural hot spring by the lake. Today two signs in English are placed next to the spring. "Swimming in the nude is not allowed" say the signs. Perhaps now the locals found their refuge being intruded. There are simply too many photographers around, some pointing not just at the swans!

Before I knew it, two of the Chinese guys crossed the bamboo fence and were in front of me taking pictures of the swans. There were plenty of swans

Ural Owl and tree eyes / 長尾林鴞和樹眼

outside the fence, but somehow they found our tiny quarters more appealing. I decided to get out of the warm water and hastily dressed myself up in the cold air fogged by rising steam of the hot spring. Snow surrounded me on all sides, including the lakefront. Soon I was on my way, driving away just as two large busloads of tourists were arriving. Next hot spring, more buses and I cared not to stop.

Indeed, in years past, to be in Hokkaido in the deep of winter has been a ritual, or even a pilgrimage, to be among nature, cranes, sea eagles, deer and fox. I rejoiced in taking pictures not only of the wildlife, but also of the scenery in the snow. Not as a professional or commercial photographer, but I simply enjoyed capturing scenes leisurely as I drove around. I usually drove only for a couple hours each day, stopping frequently to enjoy standing out in the cold breezy air. Some of my most favorite images of wildlife and nature were taken in Hokkaido snowy weather.

I always come prepared. The temperature, and this is day-time temperature, lingers around minus ten to fifteen. Bundled in layers, all the way to down pants and Sorel boots with insulated felt socks, I should be able to survive standing out. But the fingers! The challenge is to maneuver the camera, lens, focus, shutter and more, while pursuing the cranes or sea eagles in flight. Taking pictures of them on the ground has become a bore for me, having been here five times.

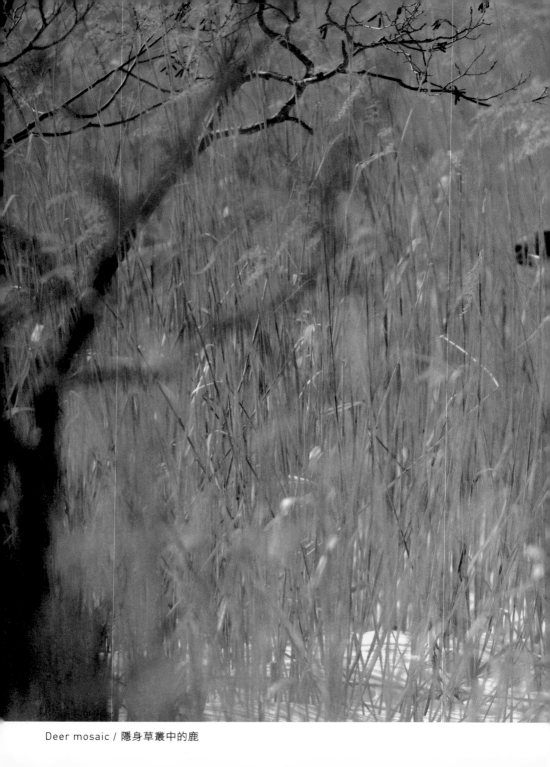

Deer mosaic / 隱身草叢中的鹿

我總是有備而來。這裡白天的氣溫在零下十到十五度左右，我的身上穿了好幾層衣服，羽絨褲，Sorel 雪靴，保暖毛襪，在外面我應該是沒有問題的。但是我的手指頭！最困難的是要一邊追空中的鶴或是海鷹，還要一邊操作相機、鏡頭、聚焦、按快門等等。只是拍牠們在陸地上已經讓我覺得沒挑戰性了，畢竟我已經來這裡五次了。

我最喜歡拍兩種海鷹，虎頭海鵰跟白尾海鵰，尤其在同一張照片捕捉到這兩種一起。單拍一隻鳥或是猛禽對我來說簡直是太簡單了。任何經驗老到、自重的野生動物攝影師應該把標準拉高一點，尤其拜現代數位相機所賜，快門速度為千分之一秒，iso 也是，長鏡頭會自動對焦，還有無限的「底片」。

難怪我一直聽到攝影師的快門像機關槍一樣。讓我回想起在戰場，古代一次只能單發一顆子彈的槍，開槍這件事顯得比較有人的感情味，而開機關槍是不需要有雙眼，也沒有感情。現今的野生動物攝影師也是一樣。我旁聽到台灣的攝影師們在聊天，一位在一天之內拍了一千七百多張的照片，其他一人超過兩千張。而這兩位都是女士。其他三位男士拍得則更多。

把照片刪掉好像是每天的例行工作，即刻得到滿足的後

I enjoy the most snapping two types of Sea Eagle, the Steller's and the White-tailed, both within the same image. Singular shots of each of these birds, or raptors, are a no-brainer as far as I am concerned. Any seasoned and selfrespecting wildlife photographer should set higher goals for himself these days, especially with the blessing of digital cameras, shutter speed into thousandth of a second, iso also into the thousands, auto-focus long focal length lenses, and unlimited "film" memory per se.

No wonder I kept hearing cameras firing off like machine gun. It reminds me of how, in battles with ancient single shot guns, killing was more personal, whereas machine gun firing needs no eyes and has no emotion attached. Today's wildlife photographer is much the same. I overheard five Taiwan photographers chatting; one had taken over 1700 frames in one day, the other over 2000. And these were the two ladies. The three men with them fired off even more exposures.

Deleting images becomes a routine, and instant gratification a given. Somehow within the last couple years, dressing up the lenses is becoming in vogue. Almost all big lenses have camouflaged clothing over them, whereas the photographers, especially Chinese ones, still dress in multiple bright and flashy colors, thus making the camera camouflage irrelevant.

果。不知道為什麼，裝飾鏡頭變成一件流行的事。幾乎所有的大砲都穿上迷彩裝，但是攝影師本人，尤其是華人，身上穿的卻是色彩鮮艷的衣服，他們為鏡頭穿上的偽裝根本派不上用場。

我想起我很崇拜的本特・伯格（Bengt Berg）所寫的一本書，他是鳥類學家也是野生動物的攝影師。這本書是在一九三一年出版，內容是關於他非常著迷拍攝的胡兀鷲（又名髭兀鷹）。

伯格在一九三零年前往喜瑪拉雅山尋找這種巨禽，他稱這趟旅程是朝聖之旅。在有經驗的老獵人的幫助下，他在很高的山溝裡找到髭兀鷹的窩。但他的相機跟裝備不夠先進到可以讓他拍攝。因此他回到歐洲去購買更好的相機跟配備。

他再次回到山溝的髭兀鷹窩，利用熱氣球的籃子跟飛機用的纜線，伯格把自己掛在山溝上，這次他成功地帶回了稀有珍貴的髭兀雛鷹照片。他把玻璃板放進相機，就蹲在那離鳥窩幾公尺遠的籃子裡好幾個鐘頭，又高又危險，好不容易才等到鳥媽媽帶著鮮肉回來餵食幼鳥。

「我拍了兩張曝光十五秒的，這是玻璃板可以浸泡的最長時間。其中的一張（在書中）很清晰。另外一張鳥的頭部

White-tailed eagles / 白尾海鵰

I remember reading with great respect and admiration a book written by Bengt Berg, a noted Swedish ornithologist and wildlife photographer. The entire book, published in 1931, is about his obsession with photographing the Bearded Vulture, or Lammergeier. It is worthy of recounting here.

Berg went to the Himalayas in search of the gigantic bird around 1930, calling the journey a pilgrimage. With help from an old hunter, he found a nest of the Bearded Vulture high up among some ravines. Limitations in his camera and equipment stopped him from recording his discovery. He thus returned to Europe to procure a better camera and equipment.

Getting back to the ravine and the nest, Berg suspended himself in a balloon

是模糊的。就像難看的羅曼史，我在恐懼與悲苦中搖擺。影像有在板子上嗎，或是我忘記關上匣子，還是忘記做哪件事，發現又太遲？我們熬夜沖片子，在臨時搭的暗房外等待，我興奮地滿身是汗。」

書裡的最後一段話真是經典，「最後，幫我沖片子的人拿著裝板子的托盤走出來，臉上表情看起來很平靜，壓在我心中的那塊大石頭終於可以放下了。我知道我在山溝上看到的是什麼，在等待的那幾個鐘頭我發誓如果這些板子洗出來的照片不好的話，我永遠也不會再碰相機了。」

書的最後柏格透露遇見這難得一見髭兀鷹的興奮與焦慮。陳述著人類對攝影，對鳥所付出的時間；與今日攝影師的態度大不相同！數位攝影給了我們更好的掌控能力，也給

White-tailed and Steller's Sea Eagles / 白尾海鵰和虎頭海鵰

basket using airplane cables, and successfully brought back some of the rarest pictures of the Bearded Vulture up close with newborn chicks. Using glass plates refilled into his camera, he squatted for hours just a couple of meters away from the nest up high and in precarious position until the time the mother bird returned with fresh meat to feed its young.

"I made two shots of fifteen seconds, which is as long as I could dip the plates. One of them, shown here (in the book) is sharp. In the other one, the bird's head was blurred. It was like a trashy romance – I swayed between fear and sorrow. Was the image there on the plate, or did I forget to close the cassette cover or any one of the things that one only notices when it is too late? I perspired completely with excitement, as we developed the film overnight and waited outside the make-shift dark room."

The last paragraph of the book is the killer. "In the end, my film developer with the plates in a tray came out and seeing his peaceful expression, a heavy weight was lifted from my heart. That I knew, with what I had seen above (on the cliff), and had sworn in these hours of waiting, that in case not one of those plates were good, that I would never hold a camera again."

The final words in Berg's book revealed the excitement and anxiety during this chance meeting of a lifetime with the Lammergeier. It is a statement about the bird, as much as about photography and human dedication of the time -

了我們及時的回應，但是同時它也奪走了等待的焦慮，還有得來不易的滿足。科學與科技已經改變了我們的價值觀以及怎麼去欣賞一件事情。

讓我透漏我怎麼看待攝影。在一九七零年早期我接觸到 *Nikon FTN* 時就帶有電動卷片器，但我從來都是定在單發，也只有將它當單發卷片用。直到今天我還是維持這原則，把每個快門都當成是特別的，很親密的一刻，拍每一張照片都好像用珍貴的底片一樣。我在兩千零六年，也是十年前才轉用數位相機拍攝，當時底片已經過時了。我是個忠誠也有些浪漫的人，至少在攝影這件事上。幾乎我所有的相機都殘舊保養的完好，陳列在香港鶴咀的攝影工作室。

今年俄國東邊西伯利亞的浮冰並沒有像往年一樣如時漂到北海道。也許是地球暖化，浮冰偶爾才出現。我坐的船只遊走在港口內，開個幾公里來娛樂大批到來的遊客。冷凍的魚被丟進海裡餵海鷹，好讓攝影師可以拍個痛快。

拍了約二十分鐘，手臂酸了，我放下 *300* 釐米的鏡頭。坐下來欣賞海鷹，我注意到虎頭海雕，體型算大，羽翼展開後很長，轉一圈需要比較大的空間跟時間，就像大卡車需要大一點的迴轉半徑。正因如此，牠動作比白尾海雕慢，也比較難在水裡抓到魚。我很滿意拍到幾張照片，在

an abject insult to today's fast-track photographer! While digital photography puts us in better control of the situation, rewarding us with instant gratification, yet at the same time it deprives us of the anxiety of suspense and the satisfaction of a hard-won battle. Science and technology have indeed changed forever our value and appreciation.

I have to reveal my take on photography. Though I have used motor-drive since picking up the Nikon FTN in the early 1970s, I've always fixed the drive as single shot, using it strictly as a winder. Today I still maintain that principle, treating each push of the shutter like a special and intimate moment, using up each frame like rare resources, similar to each exposure of film in the old days. I did not turn digital with my photography until sometime in 2006 ten years ago, when film was rendered obsolete. I am a loyal and somewhat romantic person, at least to my camera and photography. Almost all my cameras, maybe two dozen of them, are still kept well and on display in my photo studio at Cape D'Aguilar in Hong Kong.

This year the ice pack, breaking off from the Siberian east coast of Russia, did not arrive in Hokkaido as it did in years past. Perhaps due to global warming, the ice packs are here now only intermittently, being absent more frequently. So the boat in which I went out to sea only motored around inside the harbor, and sailed out only for a couple of kilometers just to make a round to entertain the tourists who are now arriving in swarms in buses. The frozen fish thrown

同一個畫面裡兩種鳥都有。

日落前的那段時間一定是留給鶴的。我的喜悅是來自拍到牠們在飛的樣子。拍在空中成對的鶴已經變成我最喜歡的事。在陸地上拍到這種優雅的鳥已經不是個挑戰了，一成不變的照片，連攝影初學者也在拍求愛舞蹈中的鶴。畢竟，日本攝影師林田恆雄曾拍攝過的正在跳舞的鶴，並刊登在一九八三年的美國國家地理雜誌，那些照片訂下了很高的標準，即使是數位相機年代也難達到那種境界。

在雪中站了好幾個鐘頭，手指雙腳受凍的痛苦終於有了回報，拍攝到美麗的鶴跟海鷹讓我滿是歡喜。回到安藤與 Shinobu 溫暖舒適的民宿，在壁爐旁暖暖我凍壞的手指與雙腳。

冬天大批的攝影師湧入，安藤多聘用了好幾個助理跟著他活動。現在，要在旺季訂到房間變得很困難了，而這裡總共也只有六間房，有的訂房甚至在一年前就訂下了。這裡的北海道已經成為我冬天休憩的地方。這趟是我第五次來這裡，當然也不會是最後一趟。安藤的牆上有我在二零一三年寫的文字，最後一句說到我即將回到這裡。是的，中國人來了，我也是其中的一位！

into sea to feed the sea eagles availed the photographers to take pictures to their hearts' content.

After twenty minutes or so of shooting, my arms got sore and I put down my camera with a 300mm lens. While sitting back to enjoy the flight of the eagles, I noticed that the Steller's Eagle, being much larger in size and with longer wing span, required more room and time to turn a circle, similar to a big truck with a wider turning radius. With that as hindrance, it maneuvers a bit slower than the White-tailed Sea Eagle and is less successful in fetching the fish over water. I felt gratified to capture several images of both types of sea eagles in the same frame.

The evenings, just before sunset, were always reserved for the Cranes. Again my only joy is derived from photographing them in flight. Pairing cranes in flight have become my favorite pursuit. The surety of capturing such stately birds on the ground has long ceased being a challenge. Such mundane photos, even cranes in courtship dance, should primarily be for the novice photographers. After all, the seminal images of dancing cranes taken by Japanese photographer Tsuneo Hayashida and published in a 1983 National Geographic has set a standard beyond redemption by late comers with digital cameras.

The agony of numb fingers and frozen feet derived from standing for hours in

Paring cranes / 求偶中的鶴

the snow is finally repaid by the ecstasy of some beautiful images of cranes and sea eagles. Back in the warm and comfortable lodge home of Ando and Shinobu, I nursed my fingers and my feet by the fireplace.

With the large influx of photographers during the winter, they have taken on three assistants since my last visit two years ago. It has become very difficult to book one of their six rooms during the peak season. Some reservations are made a year in advance. Their home has become my winter hiatus in Hokkaido. This is my fifth, and obviously not my last, visit. I looked at Ando's wall, at something I scripted back in the winter of 2013. The last verse promised my returning soon. Yes, the Chinese are coming, and I would be among them!

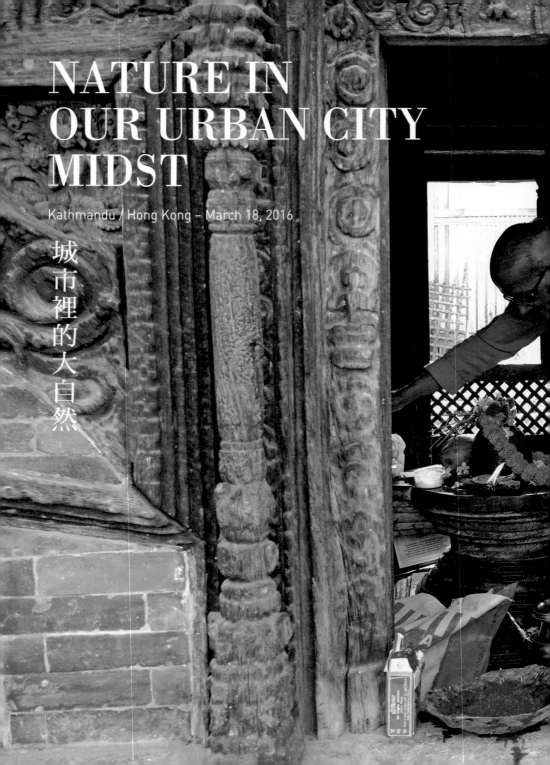

NATURE IN
OUR URBAN CITY
MIDST

Kathmandu / Hong Kong – March 18, 2016

城市裡的大自然

城市裡的大自然

「吱～吱～噠！噠！」這是蚊蟲被燒焦的聲音錯不了，它在我耳裡響個不停。隔離乘客座艙跟飛機前艙的幕簾垂落下來，這樣做是有原因的，蚊子才不會在門開開的時候飛到乘客的區域來。

從幕簾的縫隙中我看到一位空服員正揮著電蚊拍。電蚊拍打到蚊蟲時發出「嘶嘶」聲，接著一個微小的爆破聲響，此刻蚊蟲已經被消滅。外面的地還是濕濕的。達卡的雨季剛開始。孟加拉是世界上人口密度最高的國家，人口數在地球上排名第八。我從香港飛往加德滿都的飛機在這裡暫停，為了要上機下機的乘客停留。

我看見一位身穿紅色和藏紅花色長袍的西藏和尚坐在乘客當中，他坐在商務艙，隔壁坐著一位打扮精心的女士，可能是從香港來的，供養他的人。每一次的聲響一定觸動他的神經，因為代表又有生命被消滅了。也許他在思考著蚊蟲下一次的輪迴，牠會變成空服員，空服員會變成蚊子。大自然總是會找到平衡點。我的腦袋開始左右搖晃，從踏

NATURE IN OUR URBAN CITY MIDST

"Zzzz, Zzzz! Taat, taat!" - the unmistakable sound of insects being incinerated kept buzzing into my ears. The curtains were drawn, separating the passenger cabin from the front part of the airplane. It was for good reason; a precaution so that the mosquitoes swarming through the open door would not penetrate into the passenger area.

Through the cracks in the curtain, I could make out a male flight attendant swinging an electric racket back and forth. Thus the frying "fizz" sound as the racket hit its mark, followed by a tiny popping noise as the insect met its demise. Outside, the ground was wet. The rainy season had just started in Dhaka. Bangladesh is one of the most densely populated countries of the world, with a population ranking 8th on the planet. Our plane was making a stop to drop off and pick up passengers as I flew from Kathmandu to Hong Kong.

Among us passengers, I could see a Tibetan monk, in red and saffron robe, sitting in Business Class, next to a welldressed lady, probably his supplicant from Hong Kong. The monk tightened his face every time the fizzing noise

入印度大陸後我便開始有這習慣。

這景象把我的思緒帶回到前兩天我在加德滿都的時光。我住在一個靠近布達納特寺廟附近的精品旅館，布達納特寺廟有著一個很大的圓錐佛塔，被聯合國教科文組織認定為世界文化遺產，也是朝聖者在這城市活動的中心。上一次來到這裡差不多是一年前，去年的四月二十五日，就在我要飛離的時候，災難發生，強大的地震襲擊尼泊爾。當然我的班機被取消。這次大自然對我還好，沒有意外受傷，至少還沒有。

我是尼泊爾經濟論壇裡的演講者跟會議成員，會議討論喜馬拉雅的未來。*Nirupama Rao* 是印度的前外交部長，她也參加此次會議，我跟她聯繫過但是從沒見過面。我對她即將出版的書非常有興趣，書裡講的是中國與印度在一九四九年到一九六二年的蜜月期。

我在論壇上的主題是這區域的水資源，我去過好幾條河流的源頭，它們都從西藏高原開始漫長的路程一路到出海口。天然的水資源正被消耗殆盡，有時候是被人類濫用。人類用不只一種方式去掠奪大自然，大自然是會反撲的，也許會來得凶猛，剝奪我們一直習以為常的資源。是時候要控制我們的行為了，為我們好，也為未來的世代。

sounded. Each sound must touch his nerves, signaling that another sentient being was being immolated. Perhaps he was thinking that, in the insect's next incarnation, it would become the attendant, and the attendant in turn becomes the mosquito. Nature tends to also offer some equilibrium and balance. Yes, I started wagging my head from side to side in concurrence, having adopted this habit from the Indian continent.

The scene brought my thoughts back to the last two days in Kathmandu. I stayed at a boutique hotel by the Boudha, the big conical pagoda which is a UNESCO world heritage site and center of pilgrim activities in the city. The last time I was there was almost a year ago, on April 25 when disaster struck. The devastating earthquake hit Nepal just as I was about to fly out. Of course my exit was suspended. This time, nature had been kinder to me; no mishaps, at least not yet.

At the Nepal Economic Forum, I was among speakers and panelists discussing the future of the Himalayas. Also there was Nirupama Rao, former Indian Secretary of Foreign Affairs, whom I had communicated with but never met. I am hugely interested in her upcoming book about the honeymoon period between China and India from 1949 to 1962.

My focus at the Forum however was on the water resources of the region, having been to several river sources which all begin their long journey to the

Offering to Birds / 餵養鴿子的女孩

sea from the Tibetan plateau. Our natural reservoirs are being depleted, used and at times abused by mankind. In more ways than one, nature has been robbed. Nature would fight back, perhaps in even more brutal ways, by depriving us of a resource we have long taken for granted. It is time we reign in our behavior, for our own good as well as for the sake of future generations.

While at the Boudha, I saw large flock of pigeons on the sacred ground. Both Buddhists and Hindi are very kind to animals, and they make offerings to animals as well as to deities. Yet nature can still be punishing, like the tremor that rocked the Himalayan kingdom last year. My thoughts momentarily went back to Hong Kong.

CERS Tai Tam Center and our Shek O 1939 Exhibit House are both on the south side of Hong Kong Island, barely 30 minutes from city center. Ten pots of tree cordon off our Shek O house from a village alley. Five of these sevenfoot banyans have bird's nests in them. And when I left, they all had new residents, taking up their quarters within the last twelve months since I bought these plants. They are certainly more welcome than the wasp hive across from our back alley.

Over in Tai Tam, I could observe from our treehouse flocks of Black-eared Kites, the maritime raptors of our region, perform spring time courtship dances in the sky. The male, I presume, would shoot down at a female as if

在布達納特的時候我看到一大群鴿子在那聖潔的地面上。佛教徒跟印度教徒都對動物很友善，他們會奉獻供品給神明也會給動物。然而大自然卻還是可以很無情的，就像去年地震震撼整個喜馬拉雅王國。我的思緒瞬間的回到香港。

CERS 大潭中心跟我們石澳的 1939 展示屋都在香港島的南方，離市中心約三十分鐘。我們用十個盆栽樹當作石澳房子跟小巷弄間的籬笆。五顆七英尺高的榕樹上有鳥巢。我離開的時候，這些鳥巢都有了新住戶，我買這些樹還不到十二個月。牠們肯定比後面小巷對面的黃蜂巢還受歡迎。

在大潭的樹屋上我可以觀看到一群黑耳鳶，是這區域的海上猛禽，春天的時候會在空中跳求偶舞。公的，我猜，會衝向母的好像要攻擊牠，被鎖定目標的母黑耳鳶會扇動牠的翅膀閃避。最近一定有哪一對在我們的松樹上高掛鳥巢，當作牠們的新家。

好難相信我們的花園跟海濱居然會是一個天然又多樣的野生動物園。這裡有螳螂，甚至有竹節蟲；青蛙跟蝌蚪；烏龜、松鼠，還有很多蛇，有些還有毒。蛞蝓，蝸牛，蛾季節到的時候這裡也很多。有兩次我的狗被刺蝟刺到鼻子，回到家裡哇哇大叫。我們設的相機也常常捕捉到野豬的身

Floral offering / 供奉的花

attacking, while the prospective mate would flap her wings in an attempt to side-step the advance. One couple recently must have taken over a former nest high up on our pine tree.

It seems almost surreal that our garden and ocean front would be a natural zoo of wildlife diversity. There are praying mantis and even walking sticks, frogs and toads, turtles, squirrels and plenty of snakes, some poisonous. Slugs, snails, and moths can also be abundant depending on the season. Twice my dog came home whining with a quill from a porcupine in her muzzle. Our camera trap has frequently provided evidence of wild boar, the culprits

影，牠是破壞我們菜園、木瓜跟菠蘿蜜的首要罪犯。

在岸邊的海洋生物也成為我們晚餐的菜色。青蟹、花蟹，還有馬蹄蟹，海膽跟海參，蛤蠣跟淡菜，墨魚和魷魚，石斑魚和鯛魚，大小蝦，有兩次我們還捕到了龍蝦。近年來海洋變化帶來的警示，在夏季，連熱帶魚像 Nemo 都來了。

我在加德滿都看到了一個比喻我們人類的壁畫。是的，大自然是我們的鄰居，不管是不是你選的，討喜的還是被討厭的；總之不管你喜不喜歡，我們最好尊重這大自然。

responsible for devastating our vegetable garden, papayas and jackfruit trees. By our shore, marine life offers up dishes for our dinner table. Green, flower, and horseshoe crab, sea urchin and sea cucumber, clam and mussel, cuttlefish and squid, grouper and snapper, shrimp, prawn and twice even lobster. With warming of the ocean in recent years, even some tropical fish like Nemo have started arriving during summer months.

A mural I saw while strolling the streets of Kathmandu is a metaphor of us humans. Yes, nature is our neighbor, chosen or dreaded, a pet or a pest. Like it or not, we had better respect it.

Digging our own roots / 壁畫：掘根的人

需要之外加點貪心

A LITTLE GREED BEYOND NEED

Palawan, Philippines – April 18, 2016

需要之外加點貪心

終於生活步調回到「老時光」，回到那慢慢地、愜意地步調。我多麼渴望這種簡單的生活。對大多數的人來說，或許會選擇去個舒適的渡假中心感受這樣的步調。我是很舒服的，相對來說，夠舒服了，珍惜回到那種日子，那種簡單的村莊，住在簡單的竹屋裡。

對，這裡沒有自來水，甚至常常斷電。但是心理上我有預期，這裡就是這樣，我們祖先也曾經過過這樣的生活。不，這不是 *Outward Bound*（國際外展非營利組織）。我很感激我們有井水用，只需要一個水桶跟繩子就有水。芒果跟椰子從空而降，散落在我四周，這是件多棒的事。我喜歡日落時休息，日出而起。尤其是當我在海面的漁船上。

只要搭幾個鐘頭的飛機跟車程，我就可以穿越兩個世界，回到兩個世紀前，從香港忙碌的生活到菲律賓南方巴拉望的農村。這個兩個地方我都住在海邊，兩個非常不同的海邊。

A LITTLE GREED BEYOND NEED

Finally life has gone back to the "old" normal, where time is slow and days are long. How I yearn for such moments of back to basic living. Others may go on vacation at a resort to feel the change in pace, and in comfort. I too, am in comfort, relative comfort, adequate comfort, cherishing going back in time, to a simple village in a simple bamboo house.

Yes, there is no running water, and even electricity can be cut off at any moment. But mentally I came prepared, taking that as a matter of fact, just as how our forefathers had lived. No, this is not Outward Bound. I am thankful that we have well water, just a bucket and rope away. How wonderful to have mangoes and coconuts dropping from the air, left and right, all around me. I enjoy turning in when the sun sets, waking up at the first shade of light. Even more so, if I am on a fishing boat in the open sea.

I can transcend two worlds, and two centuries, between the jet set city of Hong Kong and the farm country of Palawan in the southern Philippines, all within a matter of hours, by flight and car. In both places, I live by the sea, but a very different sea.

有些人可能會覺得這裡很落後或原始，但是這種生活品質總是很吸引我，更別說它的生活物價。對，生活是重點，我在這裡非常有活力。現代摩登的網友提倡健康的生活，養生飲食，有些甚至吃素，到健身房運動，做瑜珈，打坐冥想，讓心靈平靜，消除焦慮，這些都是在城市裡追求物質、快步調生活的副產品。在這裡我的焦慮很少，除了很悠閒的問道什麼時候我還可以再出海之外。

我注意到我那三位百歲的「老」朋友跟好幾位九十幾歲的友人，沒有一個過著那樣的生活，做那樣的運動或是所謂的健康飲食。除了陳文寬，他每天早上會在 *Nordic Track* 的跑步機上走五十分鐘以外。但是他到現在每天都還會喝上一兩罐啤酒，配著洋芋片。人們往往會忘記，醫生也方便地忽略，追求健康的執著可能變成一種壓力呵。當然適當的關注也許是必須的。

在這裡簡單多了，健康的生活，值得這麼生活。好啦，我承認也不是完全這麼簡單。跟陳文寬一樣，我現在正喝著啤酒吃著洋芋片。這些東西都是開了一個鐘頭的車到 *Puerto Princesa* 城市裡買回來的，為了買這些東西可是又增加了一些碳足跡。這附近買不到這些東西。

想要體驗這裡的田園生活，只要透過坐漁船到海灣裡的漁市場就可以了。*JoDan* 今天早上回來時拖著三尾鮪魚，分

Others may consider such places backward or primitive; I have always been attracted by its quality of living, let alone its cost of living. Yes, living is the key word here, and I feel I am very much alive here. Today, our new set of modern netizens advocates healthy living, going on diet regimes, some even go vegetarian, exercising in gyms, with yoga and meditation to boot in order to calm and rid ourselves of anxieties, a byproduct of big city, fast life and the "more of" pursuit. Here I have few anxieties, except in a leisurely way of asking when I should go out to sea again.

I have always taken notice that among my three centenarian "buddies" and multiple nonagenarian friends, not one had lived by such exercise or diet regime. One exception may be Moon Chin, who would observe a 50minute walk on his NordicTrack each morning. He, however, still drinks a beer or two every day, with chips on the side. Surely, obsession with health can become a form of stress too, people tend to forget, and doctors conveniently also neglect. Of course a moderate and appropriate dosage of concern is probably necessary.

Here, it is simpler, both healthy and worthy living. Oh yes, I admit it may not be all that simple. After all, like Moon Chin, I am having a beer with some chips at the moment. Those amenities, however, I got by adding some carbon footprint, driving an hour to the city in Puerto Princesa to get them. Closer by, there are no such amenities.

Tuna fishermen returning to port in Palawan / 回到巴拉望碼頭的鮪魚漁夫

Idyllic life here is also manifested through a visit to the fish market by sailing into a bay with a fishing boat. JoDan returned home this morning with a small haul of three tuna fish in its hold, 10, 17 and 33 kilos each. The boat had been out to sea for four nights, and it stopped by a harbor to pick me up.

As we sailed near shore, I could see other slightly larger boats unloading their catch, lots of catch. These boats would have been away for ten days to two weeks. In fact, all boats are home-bound, as it is half-moon already. From now until pass full moon, there would be not much to catch, until the moon ebbs again with a new crescent and darkness befalls the open sea. Fish would then, again, be plentiful.

The further the distance from land, the more tuna they would catch, up to twenty or more fish in their ice-packed haul. From here they were brought on to small floats and tugged by hand to shore. Once on shore, the first round of transaction took place, with the tuna ultimately ending on the table of sushi restaurants after changing hands several times. Each of these hands would be the real profit center of the tuna trade.

Today, the fish on JoDan would yield only 1360 peso and

別是十公斤，十七公斤跟三十三公斤。這艘船已經出海四個晚上，它剛剛靠岸來接我。

當船接近岸邊時，我看到其他大一點的船正在卸貨，很多貨。這些船已經出海十天到兩個星期。事實上所有的船都要回來，因為月亮已經是半月形了。從現在到滿月，直到新月形成，黑暗降臨外海前，海裡沒有什麼東西好捕的。之後，又會有很多魚可以捕了。

離陸地越遠的地方越容易捕到鮪魚，他們會抓二十條或更多的魚用冰塊包覆運回。然後鮪魚會被移到小一點的浮筒船用手拽著上岸。一上岸後，進行第一次的交易，轉過好幾手後，最後鮪魚會出現在壽司店的桌上。鮪魚交易的利潤中心在每轉一手中形成。

今天 *JoDan* 捕的魚賣掉兩條大的，一條賣一千三百六十比索，另一條賣四千九百五十比索。額外贈送的一瓶大可樂當作是給船員的獎賞。買家不買十公斤的那尾，因為他們認為太小隻了！我們應該把它帶回去好好享受這魚排。鮪魚的價錢建構在很有趣也很錯綜複雜的壟斷利益集團買賣上。基於多層的協議，似乎每一艘船都有它們固定的，預定的買家。

五到九公斤重的一條鮪魚每公斤可以賣八十比索。二十

4950 peso for the two larger fish. Thrown in was a huge bottle of Coke to reward the crew. The fish buyer would not want the 10 kilo one, too small, it was deemed! We shall take it home to enjoy our own fish steak. The price paid for tuna is based on an interesting and intricate cartel of business. It seems each boat would have its own traditional and predetermined buyer, based on a multi-tier arrangement.

For a tuna between 5 to 19 kilos, 80 peso would be paid per kilo. Between 20 to 29 kilos, 110 peso is paid. Between 30-34 kilos, the price goes up to 150 peso. And for 35 kilos and over, 190 peso is the top range. This morning at the buying shops, I saw many tuna of sizes over 50 kilos each. Topping at close to 60 kilos, one young man would hold the tuna to bring it up to shore. Each would be weighed on a spring balance, before a paper sticker was put on the body with the exact weight.

But there was more than just weight and price, depending on a set of relationships between the buyer and seller. The price mentioned above is the cash price paid at shore. If the boat owner is willing to wait ten days for payment, the price paid per kilo goes up accordingly. For those who have taken money in advance, or in other words who are in debt to the buyer, the price paid would be significantly lower. Naturally a person in need or a gambler/ alcoholic type would have to pay interest.

到二十九公斤的，一公斤賣一百一十比索。三十到三十四公斤賣一百五十比索。三十五公斤以上賣的最貴，每斤一百九十比索。今天早上在魚舖裡看到許多超過五十公斤的鮪魚。最大的一尾快要六十公斤，是由一位年輕人捕上岸的。每一尾都會用彈簧秤秤重，然後用一張紙貼在魚身上標示著實際的重量。

除了重量跟價錢之外，還要靠買家跟賣家之間的關係來完成交易。上面提到的價錢是上岸的現金價。如果船東願意等十天再拿到錢的話，每公斤的賣價就會提高。如果事先就拿錢的，也就是說他們欠買家，他們賣的價格會少很多。很自然的有需要的人或是有賭博或酒癮的人會選這種

Jocelyn, my helper and owner of the JoDan, revealed to me that their largest catch ever was a tuna weighing 118 kilos. Usually anything reaching 120 kilos is considered the upper range of a tuna catch. Today, we only saw the biggest ones being half that size.

Noli, Jocelyn's elder brother, was made a hero some months ago. Not by size of his tuna catch, but when he caught a sea turtle by chance. With a shell of 180cm x 150cm in size and weighing over one hundred kilos, Noli decided to release the endangered animal back to sea. The local ABS−CBN Palawan television channel broadcasted the news as something worthy of note, kudos to an environmentally conscious fisherman.

While relaxing in Palawan, I contemplate about the notion that too much stimulation and attention for a person, even for a baby, can be cause for high anxiety, high expectations, and ultimately more disappointments. I, being an extremely curious person, may be a victim of such a malady, the high expectation syndrome, easy to arouse, difficult to satisfy.

What is adequate has a different definition for each person. Here in Palawan, for me the level of anxiety and expectations are low, much lower, so I feel adequate far more easily. At times, I even feel privileged. How can I not feel privileged when I spent a night at sea in our boat the HM Explorer II, with five dives in between. I was floating among coral fish, and swimming around

需要付利息的方式。

Jocelyn 我的幫傭也是 *JoDan* 的船東說，他們捕過最大的鮪魚重達一百一十八公斤。通常一百二十公斤已經是鮪魚頂尖的尺寸。不過今天我們看到最大的也只有那一半的大小。

Noli 是 *Jocelyn* 的哥哥，前幾個月成為一位英雄。不是因為他捕到鮪魚的大小，而是他意外的捕到一隻海龜。龜殼大小為一百八十公分乘一百五十公分，重量超過一百公斤，*Noli* 決定將這個瀕臨絕種的動物放回海裡。當地巴拉望的 *ABS-CBN* 電視台都播報了這則新聞，這是有著環保意識的漁夫的榮譽。

在巴拉望休息放鬆時，我思考著一個觀念，那就是給一個人過多的刺激跟關注，即使是嬰兒，都可能造成他們非常焦慮，期待過高，最後導致更多的失望。我是個非常好奇的人，有可能是這種弊病的受害者，過高期待的症候群就是很容易激起興趣，但是很不容易得到滿足。

什麼是「適當足夠」？對每個人的定義都不一樣。在巴拉望這裡，我的焦慮跟期待是低的，低很多，所以我很容易滿足。有的時候我甚至覺得我受到特別的待遇。我怎麼能不覺得自己很幸運，我在海上的 *HM Explorer II* 過夜，中

Sinbad's recycled umbrella sail / 用回收雨傘做成的風帆

star studded glittering sands, a beach filled with Star Fish. This is the real Avenue of the Stars, not in Hong Kong, or in Hollywood Boulevard. My needs are all met, and there seems no need to become greedier.

I have learned over the years that even if a journey arrives at a dead end, I should enjoy the process. Aren't all the river sources I arrived at dead ends? But in another way, they are also life springs of a beginning. Isn't life's destiny a dead end? But certainly we can, and should, enjoy the process nonetheless.

So do I want more? Yes indeed, a little greed beyond need. I am longing for another day on the boat, our own HM Explorer II outrigger boat or on a tiny sail boat I saw on the beach, and another day watching the sky pale at 5am, leading to yet another perfect sunrise, and ending with another perfect sunset.

間潛了五次水。我漂浮在珊瑚礁魚間，在滿是星星的，閃亮的沙灘邊游泳，一個有好多海星的海灘。這是一個真正的星光大道，不是在香港，也不是在好萊塢。我的需求都被滿足，似乎也沒有需要再更貪心了。

這些年來我學到即使這趟旅途帶我到一個死胡同，我還是應該很享受這過程。我所去過的河流源頭不都是末路嗎？不過另一方面，它們也是生命的起源。生命不是注定會抵達終點嗎？但是無論如何我們可以，也應該，享受這個過程。

所以我還想要更多嗎？是的，確實是，比我所需要的還要多一點點的貪心。我嚮往可以在船上再多待一天，不管在我們自己的 *HM Explorer II* 外伸支架艇，還是我在海邊看到的小帆船；我希望可以再多一天在早晨五點看著天空的魚肚白，欣賞又一個完美的日出，然後，又一個完美的日落結束這一天。

在巴拉望悠閒的一天

A DAY
OF LEISURE
IN PALAWAN

Palawan, Philippines – July 6, 2016

在巴拉望悠閒的一天

巴拉望這名字用中文發音聽起來像是「派來玩」。所以我應該有一天可以輕鬆點。今天看到的都是橘色。我的 *Omega Solar Impuse* 腕錶的錶帶是橘色的。我躺在一張我在紐約買的亮橘色吊床。今天早上喝完鮮榨柳橙汁之後，我騎著一台 *Yamaha* 特定版摩托車，全新無拋光的橘色車子出去漫遊。陽台長板凳（我用來當床的）上的睡袋，也是鮮橘色的。所有的東西除了摩托車之外都是意外，不是刻意設計的。

出於同樣的道理，我們接觸很多項目一開始也是不經意的遇見，我們介入後才有計畫。機會，會自己現身，我們只是在合適的地方跟合適的時間把握它們。也許有些讀者不介意從閱讀我做的項目中先歇息一下，聽聽我在漫長的早晨閒談些什麼。畢竟今天是巴拉望的國定假日，齋戒月。在菲律賓的南部，這假日不是只有回教徒才有，所有的人都可以休息一天。這讓步調緩慢的生活又變得更慢了一些。

A DAY OF LEISURE IN PALAWAN

Palawan in phonetic Chinese means "sent to play"（派來玩）. So I should take it easy for just a day. And I am seeing orange today. My Omega Solar Impulse watch has an orange band. I am laying in a bright orange hammock I bought in New York. Earlier this morning, I cruised in our brand new mat orange colored, special edition Yamaha motorcycle, after having my fresh-squeezed orange juice. And the sleeping bag I use on the balcony bench as my bed is, again, bright orange. All of these, however, except the motorbike, are by chance rather than by design.

By the same token, most of our projects came about first by chance, followed then by design! Opportunities manifest themselves. We simply seize them where and when appropriate. Maybe some of my readers won't mind taking a break from reading about my projects, and instead would appreciate hearing about how I shoot the breezes in a slow morning. After all, it is a public holiday here in Palawan, Ramadan that is. Here in the southern Philippines, the holiday is not just for Muslims, but everyone gets a day off. A slow life just got even slower.

雨季跟颱風季已經到了。颱風 *Butchoy* 正接近我們的西方，靠近南沙群島，讓這裡的政治風暴又添上一筆天然的風暴。新的菲律賓總統杜特蒂提供了一個新的遠景，一位很不同也很主動的總統宣布他會跟中國展開對話，即便海牙國際法庭就南海主權爭端做出有利於菲律賓的仲裁。

一個強大的政府可以交出結果，而一個很弱的最多只能給個共識。我相信現任中國政府是強大的，而菲律賓新政府也比以前的強勢。這是個不可錯過的機會。

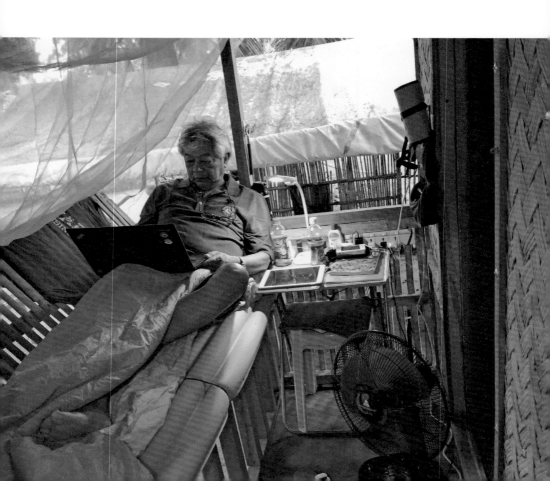

Rainy season, as well as typhoon season, has arrived. Typhoon Butchoy is looming to our west, near the Spratly Islands, adding nature's storm to a political one. The new President provides a new outlook, as Duterte, an unusually proactive president, announced that he would open dialogue with China, even if the International Court at The Hague should rule on the side of the Philippines in the dispute over the islands' sovereignty.

A strong government produces results whereas a weak one can provide at best a consensus. I believe that the current Chinese government is a strong one and the new Philippines government has a better mandate than previous ones. This is an opportunity not to be missed.

Politics is moment to moment, whereas nature is more sustainable. So let's talk more about the weather, or about our environment. I just wrote a short philosophical note as opening statement for our Myanmar natural history exhibit of freshwater aquaria, which are stocked with both indigenous and invasive fish from Inle Lake. My note seems perhaps relevant to much of the world today, so I share it here:

"Our forefather left us many treasures; knowledge gathered over millennia, and much pristine forest, blue oceans, green rivers and turquoise lakes, meadows with an abundance of wild flowers and wildlife. What are we, after one generation, leaving behind in this world for our next generation?

政治是一時的，而大自然是永續的。我們來聊聊關於氣候或是跟環境有關的話題吧。我剛剛寫了一小段哲學性的文章來當作我們緬甸自然歷史展覽的開幕詞，淡水水族館裡有茵萊湖原生魚跟外來入侵的魚，我的開幕詞也許也對應到當今的世界，所以我在這裡跟大家分享。

「我們的祖先留給我們許多寶藏，累積千年的知識，原始的森林，湛藍的海洋，綠水跟蔚藍的湖，草原上豐富的野花和野生動物。我們是誰？在這個世代過後留給接下來的世代這樣的世界。可悲的是說出來會讓我們都很羞愧。這個展覽用來提醒我們，傳承到我們手上的世界是這樣美麗，但是這個美麗世界也有可能在我們這一代被破壞，除非我們開始改變我們生活的方式，開始養護、照顧，跟修復這幾十年來我們對地球所造成的傷害。」

我的思緒暫時回到六百年前明朝第一位皇帝在位的時間。當朱元璋還是個年輕的學生和尚，一晚他很晚才回到寺廟，發現大門已經鎖上。他決定就躺在戶外，睡在地上。他寫道：

「天為羅帳地為毯
　日月星辰伴我眠
　夜間不敢長伸足
　恐怕踏破海底天」

Verbalizing it would make us all sadly ashamed. This exhibit will serve as a reminder of the beauty handed to us that would likely be ruined within our lifetime, unless we start modifying the way we live, and begin nursing and repairing the ills we have inflicted upon this earth over the last few decades."

My thoughts momentarily went back six hundred some years to the time of the First Emperor of the Ming Dynasty. When Zhu Yuanzhang was a young student monk, returning to his temple late one night, he found the gate to his monastery was closed already. He decided to sleep were he was. Laying in the open, he wrote,

"The sky my canopy and the ground my rug, the sun my company, together with the moon, stars and constellations I hug; At night I dare not too far my legs to stretch, in fear of crushing over the ocean's edge."

天為羅帳地為毯 日月星辰伴我眠 夜間不敢長伸足 恐怕踏破海底天

The future Emperor seemed to at once enjoy nature as well as prophesize, in his very daring stroke, the human impact on it. It serves as a metaphor of what we human are inflicting on the earth around us today, poking holes and creating damages all over the world.

But in less developed areas, we can still find certain pristine hidden treasures,

這位未來的皇帝好像很喜歡大自然，跟預言中說的一樣，他大膽地行為對人類是有影響的。這好像是隱喻人類對地球造成的影響，在世界各地恣意的破壞環境。

在比較未開發的地方我們還是可以找到一些被隱藏的原始珍寶，相對地還沒有被所謂的「文明化」所影響。一輩子當一個探險家，成人後的四十多年來，我很幸運有機會去到這些地方拜訪跟體驗。這些都是我最珍惜的時光，我允許自己去享受這難得的浪漫主義，這種浪漫是人與人之間難以複製的。

今天退潮的時候我走到泥灘上去看我們探險用的外伸支架艇，*HM Explorer 2*，一艘比較小，也比在緬甸的 *HM Explorer 1* 年輕的船。這是我第一次看到這艘船離水，退潮後在泥地上。旁邊有百隻，或許千隻招潮蟹在退潮的時候從洞穴裡爬出來。牠們展現橘色的螯，牠們有著一支大螯和一支迷你螯，我看見迷你的螯在大螯上揮舞著就像拉提琴一樣。這景象也讓我想到另一位中國詩人兼革命家魯迅所寫的詩：

「長將冷眼觀螃蟹，看你橫行到幾時？」

對一些我們在香港的朋友跟支持者，最近可能聽聞在大潭發生的不幸事件，關於我們在古老村莊的據點。或許這明

relatively untouched by our socalled "civilization". Being a life-long explorer, for over forty years of my adult life, I have been fortunate to visit and experience some such sites. Those times are the most precious to me, when I allow myself to enjoy that rare moment of romanticism, which human romance can hardly replicate.

At low tide today, I walked out the mud flat to visit our exploration outrigger banca boat, HM Explorer 2, a smaller and younger brother to our HM Explorer 1 in Myanmar. This is the first time I saw the boat out of water, sitting on the mud. Nearby are hundreds, perhaps thousands, of Fiddler Crab, crawling out of their hide as the water recedes. Showing off their huge orangey claws, one huge and one miniature, I watch the tiny claw playing fiddle in between the large one. The scene reminded me of yet another poem by a Chinese revolutionary author Lu Xun,

"With cold eyes I watch with slight the crab, how long can you walk sideways I await?" In Chinese, "walking sideways" means "bullying". (長將冷眼觀螃蟹，看你橫行到幾時？)

For some of our friends and supporters in Hong Kong who have been following the recent drama in Tai Tam Bay which affected our premises in an ancient village, perhaps the poem by the first Ming Dynasty Emperor also provides a metaphor for our old school house turned researcher's dorm/library. We may be

朝皇帝的詩可以做為一個隱喻，對照我們把老舊的學校改成研究員宿舍及圖書館。我們或許暫時被鎖在外面（這樣說也不對，因為我們被允許可以留在我們所擁有建築物裡），不過我們對未來還是充滿希望。

就像這裡的蟬，每天早上六點半準時唱歌，而且牠們只會在村莊這邊的屋子附近唱十五分鐘。蟬的合唱也剛好相呼應媒體上聳人聽聞的新聞誇張報導。在香港發生的小插曲是我們工作長久以來的小波折，向來我們看到需要幫助的，我們都會出手，像是很多次我們將破舊的房子整修後再加入額外的利用價值；或者是為受到威脅的野生動物發聲；以及復原被人類破壞的環境。

這次是這兩年內我來巴拉望的第五趟，但是我們的工作卻還沒真正的開始。不像朱元璋擔心伸長腳的後果，我相信我們的腳步不會在大自然裡製造新的負擔，而是跟美麗純淨的環境相呼應。

就像開頭提到巴拉望在中文聽起來像「派來玩」。所以我會試著在這裡一邊做些有意義的事，一邊做到被「派來玩」的任務。

Fiddler crab on mudflat / 泥地上的招潮蟹

momentarily locked out (not fully accurate as we are allowed to remain in all our buildings), but we continue to have high aspirations of better things to come.

Like the Cicadas here, which only sing around the village house where I am staying, for 15 minutes every day from 6:30 pm sharp. The chorus echoes how some in the media world are picking up on sensational news stories. The hiccup in Hong Kong is a hiatus from our long journey in repairing some of the ills we see around us, at various times adding value to a long dilapidated premises, or campaigning to save a threatened wildlife species, or healing the damage to environments that surround us.

This is my fifth trip to Palawan within two years, but our work is barely beginning. Unlike Emperor Zhu worrying about stretching his legs, I am confident that our legs will not poke new holes in nature, but instead will be in step with the beautiful and pristine environment around us.

As mentioned in the beginning, Palawan in phonetic Chinese is "sent to play". So I will try to live up to that while doing something worthy in the meantime.

柚木假裝棕樹

TEAK PRETENDING TO BE PALM

柚木假裝棕樹

森林很暗。舊月消退，但是新月還沒秀出他的臉來。當風平靜下來時，低聲耳語傳來：「媽，我很害怕，外面好黑。」小樹苗抬起頭來看著大樹。母親低頭看，用她的大葉手臂輕拂她的小孩。「孩子，不用擔心。假以時日你會長大，看到天空、月亮還有滿天星斗。」母親用充滿慈愛的聲音說。

當母親把頭撇開的時候，眼淚緩緩流下。在她的心裡，她無從知道自己的小孩會不會長的跟她一樣高。看著她的腰圍，一圈白色的標記，她知道自己剩下的日子不多了。「在下雨嗎，媽？」微小的聲音問。母親很快的擦掉眼淚，再次低頭看。「沒有，我的孩子，這只是幾顆星星掉下來。」她帶著微笑說。她必須要讓孩子的想像力繼續活躍。

夜漸深，雲靠近，風開始撥動。巨大的柚木葉開始大聲地揮打。母親的樹幹很堅硬，站的又直又挺面對強風。瞬間，熱帶風暴開始發威，大雨傾瀉而下。小孩還很弱

TEAK PRETENDING TO BE PALM

The forest is dark. The old moon has ebbed and the new moon has yet to show his face. There is a whisper as the wind dies down. "Mom, I am scared, it is so dark out," the tiny sapling raised his head and looked at the taller tree. Mother looked down and brushed her child with her arm of large leafs. "Child, don't worry. In time you will grow up and see the sky, the moon and even the stars," said the mother with a loving voice.

As she looked away, however, tears started dropping from her eyes. In her heart, she had no way of knowing whether her child would ever grow up as tall as she. Looking down at her own girth, marked with a white ring, she knew her own days were numbered. "Is it raining, mom?" The small voice asked. The mother quickly wiped her tears and looked down again. "No my child, it is just a few stars falling," she said with a gentle smile. She must keep her child's imagination alive.

As the night grew older, cloud moved in and the wind stirred up. The giant teak leafs started waving and flapping noisily. But mother has a hard trunk, standing firm and straight against the wind. In a moment, a tropical storm

小，緊緊地抓住媽媽的腳。一些棕櫚葉，還彎大片的開始掉下來。母親很快的將一些葉子用來幫助遮蓋她的小孩。她想，也許用棕櫚葉偽裝，她的小孩有可能會被放過一馬。不過這當然只是妄想，因為有一天她的小孩會長的比棕櫚樹還高大。「他長得越快，也代表他會早一點被砍掉！」。

自從四年前伴侶被一群筏木者砍掉之後，母親就以寡婦的身分獨自扶養小孩四年了。最近砍樹的速度加快，因為消息傳開不久後這裡的筏木將被禁止。不過這消息已經傳好多遍了，每謠傳一次就刺激一回砍樹的速度，跟時間賽跑。當然長的最高壯的那些是首選。好幾十年，樹，尤其是柚木長的正好的時候被砍，從來都沒有機會可以再長的更老，像古代時候那樣的老森林。電鋸取代了斧頭，更是加快森林消失的速度。現在甚至連大象都在慢慢地減少中，重型機械跟拖拉機取代了牠們。

母親從小就認識的河流跟小溪從青綠色變成泥黃色，很像這裡的 *Burmese tea* 緬甸奶茶顏色一樣，或是近期改稱的 *Myanmar tea*。表層土壤被沖刷，雨季時從山上被山洪帶下山，沖到依洛瓦底江再往海裡去。碎片殘骸跟漂流木隨著河流往下漂，沿岸的筏夫跟村民會去撿拾它們，連做一頓簡單的飯都需要用上這些，特別是住在茅草屋跟竹屋的人。

kicked up and rain started pouring down. The child was still weak and tiny, and braced himself closely to the foot of his mother. Some palm leaves, rather large pieces, began falling. Mother quickly brushed some aside to help cover her child. She thought, perhaps with the camouflage of a palm, her child would be spared. But of course that was wishful thinking, as the child would someday outgrow the palm. "The faster he grows, the sooner he will be cut down!"

Mother has been raising her child as a widow for four years, ever since her mate was taken down by a troupe of loggers. Cutting had accelerated recently as word had spread that soon there would be a ban in logging. But that story had been told many times over, each time instigating a new round of speed logging, racing for time. Of course, the tallest and strongest would go first. For decades, trees, in particular teak, had been felled at their prime, never being allowed to grow old like in the old days in the old forest. Chainsaws replaced the axe, further speeding up the process of the forest's demise. Now, even the elephants were gradually disappearing, replaced by heavy machines and tractors.

The river and stream that Mother knew as a child had turned from turquoise to muddy yellow, resembling what was known in this land as Burma tea, and more recently, as Myanmar tea. Top soil was washed off, carried by torrents from the mountain during the monsoon season, joining the Irrawaddy on its

竹子是給窮人用的，木頭是給一般人，柚木是給富豪，或是那些假裝是富豪的。在以前，部落酋長，甚至是山裡跟森林裡的族人都用得起柚木來蓋房子。那是母親還小的年代。她看過英國人，她偶然聽到有人叫他們「*Sahib*」，帶領一隊隊的男人跟大象進入她的森林。很快的，樹像骨牌一樣一個著接一個倒下，沒多久她的祖父祖母還有她的父母親都走了。接下來是她這一代，她們根本沒有機會去感受生命，更別說可以步入老年了。

木材以前都是被放在筏或舢板上，然後順著洛瓦底江往下漂流；或者是被放在那些被稱為「平台」的上面，然後綁在拖船上被運走。現在更大更快的舢舨跟船上可以堆疊著很高的木材，從貯木場往河的低處途中有好幾站停靠點。這些木材，母親已過逝的親戚們，要被送往國外的市場。

夜空裡終於閃電交加，隨後跟著雷的巨響，接著雨也停了，至少在這個夜晚雨是停了。小孩從依偎在母親的影子下走出來再度往上看。瞬間蟋蟀開始鳴叫，很快的森林充滿昆蟲的合唱。一隻飛蛾偷聽到一些筏木人在營地裡圍著營火聊天。

「八卦說這營區這周末會被撤掉，」蟋蟀說。「這國家換了新政府上來突然間所有的筏木都被禁止。」牠又說。消息在這群夜晚歌唱的歌手間傳的很快。一隻蝙蝠也幫忙傳

way to the ocean. Debris and driftwood floated down with the current, being collected by rafters and villagers along the river. Such tidbits were still up to the task of a simply cooked meal, especially for those living in plain thatched and bamboo houses.

Bamboo is for the poor, wood for the common folks and teak for the regal, or those who pretend to be regal. In the old days, tribal chiefs, even mountain and forest tribesman, could afford teak for their homes. That was when Mother was a child. She had seen the British man, someone she overheard called 'Sahib,' leading troupes of men and elephants into her forest. Soon trees started falling like dominoes, and before long her grandfather and grandmother, as well as her parents, were gone. Next came her generation, they were never given a chance to live out their lives, let alone to reach old age.

Logs used to float down the Irrawaddy as rafts or barges, or in what were called flats, tied to a tugboat. Today larger and faster barges and boats with logs stacked high go from timber yards to multiple destinations lower down the river. These logs, dead relatives of Mother, were all destined for foreign markets.

A last bright lightning in the night sky followed by a huge thunder clap spelled the end of the rain, at least for this night. The child snuggled out of his mother's shadow and looked up again. Momentarily a cricket started chirping,

消息，牠幫腔說：「所有的貯木場，有些人稱柚木墓地也即將被關掉」。聽到這消息，母親轉頭向上天禱告。「請讓我的孩子長大。讓他長的又高又壯，讓他在我們身旁，心愛的森林裡繼續成長，」母親靜靜地在心裡唸著，當她每次微笑，就像是臉上出現的微小皺紋。此刻她揮著她的大葉將孩子身上的棕櫚撥開。

小柚樹苗剛睡醒，問：「媽媽，怎麼了？」。「沒事，回去睡你的覺吧，寶貝！」母親用甜美的聲調回答，開始輕輕唱著催眠曲直到夜深。

and soon the forest was filled with a chorus of insect songs. It seemed a moth had overheard some loggers chatting over a bonfire at their camp.

"Gossip has it that the camp would be pulled this weekend," said the cricket. "There has been a change of government in the country and suddenly all logging is banned," he added. The message was relayed quickly among the army of night singers. The bat who helped relay the message chimed in "All timber yards, what some called the Cemetery of Teak, will also be closed,". Upon hearing this, Mother turned her head to heaven and made a prayer. "Please let my child grow. Let him be strong and be sturdy, so he would rise again with the beloved forest around us," Mother whispered quietly from her heart, as a smile broke out as a tiny wrinkle on her face. At that same moment, she moved her branch of gigantic leafs and brushed off the palm covering her child.

The teak sapling just woke up from his sleep and asked, "Mother, what's the matter?" "Nothing is the matter, just go back to your sleep, baby!" Mother answered with a sweet tone, and began singing a lullaby into the darkness.

國家圖書館出版品預行編目 (CIP) 資料

自然緣份 / 黃效文著.
-- 初版 . -- [新北市]：依揚想亮人文 , 2016.11
面； 公分
ISBN 978-986-93841-0-0（平裝）

855   105019550

自
然
緣
份

作者·黃效文 ｜ 發行人·劉鋆 ｜ 責任編輯·王思晴 ｜ 美術編輯·Rene Lo ｜ 法律顧問·達文西個資暨高科技法律事務所 ｜ 出版社·依揚想亮人文事業有限公司 ｜翻譯 · 依揚想亮人文事業有限公司 ｜ 經銷商·聯合發行股份有限公司 ｜ 地址·新北市新店區寶橋路 235 巷 6 弄 6 號 2 樓 ｜ 電話·02 2917 8022 ｜ 印刷·禹利電子分色有限公司 ｜ 初版一刷·2016 年 11 月（平裝）｜ ISBN·978-986-93841-0-0 ｜定價·400 元 ｜ 版權所有 翻印必究 ｜ Print in Taiwan